Books by Helena Stone

Dublin Virtues

Patience

Single Titles

Scenes from Adelaide Road

I0570594

Patience

ISBN # 978-1-78686-131-3

Interior text design by Claire Siemaszkiewicz

Pride Publishing

Published in 2017 by Pride Publishing, Newland House, The Point, Weaver Road, Lincoln, LN6 3QN, United Kingdom.

Pride Publishing is a subsidiary of Totally Entwined Group Limited.

Dublin Virtues

PATIENCE

HELENA STONE

Dedication

Dermot, this one's for you!
Thank you for making me look better than I actually am
and for not losing your patience or your sense of humor.

Chapter One

Here we go again. Xander stared as the man he'd spent a few sweaty hours with walked away without a backward glance. He closed the front door as softly as he could before his guest reached the stairs leading to the street. With a sigh, he rested his forehead against the smooth wood. Weariness crept into his bones, swiftly followed by anger. He squeezed his hands into fists and raised one before lowering it again. The middle of the night was not the time to slam his hand against the door, no matter how frustrated he was.

"Don't hold back on my account."

Xander's heart stuttered at the unexpected voice coming from behind.

Shit. Bollix. Fuck. Xander raised his hand again and forcefully hit the door, immediately regretting the action as pain seared through his arm.

"Another one bites the dust, I see."

Xander spun around, fury and embarrassment battling for dominance, as he glared at his housemate, and most of the time best friend, Eric.

"What are you doing up at this ungodly hour?" Xander didn't try to keep the frustration from his voice, in the hope that an attack would hide the discomfort he experienced.

"I've got no idea. Give me a minute. What could possibly have me awake at this time of night?" Eric remained expressionless as he stared at Xander. "It may have been the bed frame rhythmically hitting the wall between our bedrooms earlier. Or the noises from the shower. Or maybe it's because you still haven't done anything to stop the hinges on your door from squeaking every time it opens or closes. Take your pick."

"I..." Xander swallowed, biting down on a smart retort as he realized his housemate had a point. He glanced at Eric's face and was just in time to see his features relax and a small smile tug at his lips.

"Cat got your tongue? It's not very often you're lost for words." A smirk appeared on Eric's face but the sting had gone out of his tone and Xander allowed himself a small sigh of relief.

"I'd love to know what's up with you, though. You've always been popular, but I've never known you to slut around like this in the past. Is this a new thing? Something you developed while I was overseas?"

Xander opened his mouth to give a flippant reply then pressed his lips together again. He might not like to admit it, but once again, Eric had a point. Instead of answering, he shrugged and shook his head, hoping it would be enough to make Eric drop the subject and allow them to go back to bed. It was three in the morning. Apart from the opportunity for a few hours of undisturbed sleep, Xander couldn't come up with a possible positive spin to put on his *guest's* early departure.

"Let's have a cup of tea, seeing as we're both up, anyway." Eric didn't wait for an answer but turned and walked toward the kitchen.

Xander watched his friend's retreating form and sighed before reluctantly following him. He didn't want to have this conversation but he'd known it was coming. It had been six weeks since Eric had returned from Canada where he had worked and lived for two years. It had made sense to offer his spare room to the man who'd been his best friend since they'd both been ten years old, just as it had seemed logical to tell Eric there was no need for him to hurry about finding a place of his own. Reasonably priced accommodations were next to impossible to find in Dublin unless you were prepared to live in a shoebox, and Xander had more than enough space in his apartment. Of course,

Xander hadn't stopped to consider what having a live-in guest would mean for his nocturnal adventures. He sighed as he realized he wouldn't be able to fob Eric off with half-answers and evasions either. The man knew him too bloody well.

When Xander dragged himself into the kitchen, the kettle was on and Eric had two mugs waiting on the counter.

"It's still the middle of the night." Xander figured it was worth a try. "You need to get up for work in a few hours. We could have this conversation later today." *Or not at all.* Xander didn't hold out any hope for that possibility.

Eric turned from the counter and looked at Xander. All signs of levity were gone and replaced by concern. "It's okay. I'm wide awake now, anyway, and I've been trying to find an opening for this talk for days. Might as well take advantage of the opportunity."

"I don't really want to—"

"Leave it, Xander. You know me well enough to realize I'm not going to let it drop, now that I've opened my mouth."

Xander nodded. Eric rarely dropped an issue after he'd broached it—something he used to admire in him. He sat down at the kitchen table and waited in silence for the kettle to boil and for Eric to make their tea. Only when they both had a steaming mug in front of them did Eric speak again.

"So, what is going on with you? It's shocking how much you've changed in only two years. If I remember correctly, you used to say how you couldn't see the attraction in one-night stands."

Bollix. This was not what Xander had prepared himself for. He'd been ready for a speech about him being a selfish bastard. He was happy and willing to apologize for not taking Eric into consideration when he brought people home and took them to his bed. He didn't want to talk about *why* he did it, though.

"I haven't been that bad." As he said the words Xander realized that not only did he sound childish, he also wasn't being honest.

"Really?" Eric raised an eyebrow. "You reckon ten one-night stands in six weeks is unremarkable?"

"You've been keeping count?" Indignation swept through Xander.

"I told you, your nighttime activities have been hard to miss or ignore."

Indignation evaporated and was replaced by shame. "I'm sorry. I guess I'm still getting used to sharing my house. I'll try and be quieter in the future."

"No!" Eric shook his head. "That's not why we're having this talk. I want to figure out what happened to you. Where's the Xander I used to know and what have you done with him?"

Xander hesitated. He understood exactly what Eric meant but didn't want to consider the question or try to formulate an answer so he attempted to buy himself some time. "What do you mean? I'm the same Xander I always was."

"No, you're not." Eric almost sounded sad. "If you had ten casual hook-ups in the decade between coming out and the day I left for Canada it was a lot. Do you remember that talk we had before I went? I could have sworn you told me you were ready to settle down, be responsible and hopefully find a long-term partner. That is what you said, right?"

Xander could only nod.

"And you did some of it. You established yourself as an artist and illustrator and managed to snap up your own apartment. So what happened to creating stability in your love life?"

Xander picked up his mug and took a sip of the still too-hot tea, buying himself some more time as well as a burned tongue.

"Hey," Eric's voice was soft and gentle, "it's me you're talking to. Remember me? I'm your friend. There's nothing you can tell me that would make me love you less. Just spit it out."

"Men." Xander stopped talking and swallowed. "Men happened. If there is anybody our age out there looking for a relationship I've yet to find him. I tried, trust me. I really did." He thought back and had no problem remembering how it had all unfolded. He'd gone out, and more often than not, he'd end up talking to a man he liked. They'd spend the evening chatting, drinking, flirting and laughing and by the end of it there never seemed to be a good reason not to bring him home.

"Those first few times, I hoped that sex would lead to breakfast together, an exchange of phone numbers followed by more dates, more nights and maybe a relationship." Xander was surprised to find it still hurt. "It never worked out like that. Those men would leave as soon as we'd both gotten off. Some might take a shower first, but with one or two exceptions they never stayed long enough for scrambled eggs."

The few times a man had stayed until morning, the atmosphere had been so uncomfortable even Xander had been glad when his hook-up had decided it was time to leave. And all of that didn't even take into consideration the selfish bastard he'd brought home three months or so ago. For that man, it hadn't been enough to just leave. He'd humiliated Xander first. Anger bubbled up again as Xander remembered how he'd ended that night crying in the shower — disgusted with himself and angry with the world.

"I guess you could say I gave up on the whole idea. After a few months, I'd gotten the message. I was good enough for some hot sex but not interesting enough for anything beyond that. So now I just take what I can get. There's no point in continuing to set myself up for disappointment." Xander clamped his mouth shut. He wasn't going to go on and tell Eric about that prick who'd made him cry. Just because Eric was his best friend didn't mean Xander was happy to share all his humiliations with him.

Xander put his now empty mug on the table and rested his hands next to it. When Eric reached across and squeezed one of them, Xander realized he'd been far less successful at keeping the hurt out of his voice than he'd hoped.

"Are you at least enjoying these one-night stands?"

Eric's question made perfect sense, and yet it pulled Xander up short. He'd never asked himself that, and now that the issue had been raised, he wasn't sure it was something he wanted to pursue.

"It's fun while it lasts." Xander realized he once again said a lot less than he might have. He didn't want to admit these nights left him feeling increasingly empty and alone, and he definitely didn't want to tell Eric that his confidence had all but disappeared once it had become clear that the men he encountered never saw him as relationship material. These days, picking up men was almost a necessity—a confidence boost he needed to convince himself that he was still attractive in the eyes of others. If he wasn't good enough for a relationship, he needed the reassurance that he could at least still connect on some level.

"Have you ever considered that you might be going about it the wrong way?" Eric sounded almost hesitant when he spoke.

"What do you mean?"

"I don't know." Eric shrugged. "Seems to me that if you take every man you meet straight to your bed they could be excused for concluding you're not in the market for a relationship." Eric grinned. "And now I sound just like my father when he tries to talk some sense in to my baby sister."

Xander stared at his friend, trying to figure out if he could be right. "That doesn't sound right. I mean, picking up men is perfectly normal in the crowd I hang out with. Everybody does it. Some end up in a relationship, although they appear to be in the minority. Most men don't, and as far as I can tell, they're perfectly fine with that."

"How can you be sure about that?" Eric asked. "Would anybody who doesn't know you as well as I do be able to tell you're less than happy with the situation?"

Xander contemplated the question for a few moments.

"Probably not," he eventually conceded. "I don't want others to be aware of that. It's bad enough I'm clearly not relationship material. I'm not about to advertise how much I hate that."

"Don't be stupid." Anger crept into Eric's voice. "Jaysus, if I didn't see you as my brother I'd have a relationship with you myself. The problem is, you don't give people the chance to get close to you. They're probably all convinced you're only interested in a quick fuck and they're accommodating enough to give it to you."

Eric looked away as if his outburst had surprised him as much as it had shocked Xander. "I've got an idea."

"You have an idea." Xander smiled for the first time since they'd started their talk. "Why does that sentence scare the shit out of me? Oh...wait, it's all coming back to me. In the past, one of your ideas led to me being stranded in the middle of Paris without any money. And then there was the time I ended up being brought home by the *gardai*."

Eric beamed back at Xander, apparently sharing Xander's relief that their conversation had taken on a lighter tone. "Nothing like the ideas I had on those occasions. Besides, the *gardai* incident had far more to do with your poor impulse control than my idea. Anyway, I wonder... Are you up for a little bet?"

"What are we betting on?" Xander wasn't sure whether or not to worry about what might be coming next.

"I bet you can't go a whole month without bringing another man home." Eric paused for a moment. "Or without going to another man's place." Eric grinned, clearly delighted with himself for closing the loophole before Xander had even spotted it.

"How's that a bet?" Xander laughed. "If I just stay at home for a month there'd be no risk of me picking anybody up."

"That would be considered cheating." Eric smiled before his expression turned serious again. "The bet would mean that you'd live your life as you always do, be your usual sociable self, with the one exception that you wouldn't have sex with anyone."

Xander sat back and stared at his friend as he considered the proposal. He and Eric had always been competitive and he was tempted just to say yes and jump into the challenge but he detested losing too much not to take his time before replying.

"Spell it out for me," Xander said. "I would still go out. I can still talk to men, and what else? Would I be allowed to kiss? Give or receive blow jobs? Is it just about lack of penetration or is there more to this bet of yours?"

"You're considering taking up the challenge then?" Eric asked.

"Yes. I think so." *After all,* Xander pondered, *given how frustrating the meaningless one-night stands have recently become, I can't imagine a month without picking anyone up being any worse.*

"Nice one." Eric's grin was almost wicked. "Here's the deal. You can date. You can kiss, but you can't get naked, so blow jobs are off the table for a month, too."

"Harsh."

"Hey, it's a bet. There's supposed to be something at stake or it wouldn't be worth it," Eric said.

"While we're on the topic of stakes, what happens if I win?" Xander hesitated before going on. "Or if I lose for that matter?"

"Oh. I hadn't thought that far ahead." Eric stared off into the distance, leaving Xander caught between excitement and apprehension. He'd already made up his mind to accept the challenge but he'd spent more than enough time around Eric to realize the man could come up with devilish ideas once he set his mind to it. Xander studied Eric's face and recognized the moment he made his decision.

"I could suggest something silly or outrageous, but I'm actually serious about this so let's keep it simple. Whoever loses takes care of the other and the house for the subsequent month. That's the cooking, cleaning, laundry, shopping, the whole shebang. How about it? Are you in?"

"Fuck, yeah. It's only one month. Easy win for me." Xander laughed and was surprised when Eric didn't join him.

"I hope you're right, mate." Eric got up from his chair and moved around the table before resting a hand on Xander's shoulder. "I really hope you're right. You haven't been yourself since I returned and I want the old you back." Eric squeezed Xander's shoulder one last time and walked on. "I'm going to see if I can't get a few more hours of sleep. You should do the same."

Xander yawned as he watched Eric return to his bedroom. Getting some shut eye sounded like a good idea.

Chapter Two

When Troy Moriarty woke up at half past six in the morning it took him a moment before he realized where he was. He turned over toward the streak of light entering his room through the narrow gap between the curtain and the windowsill. Every morning over the past three months had been the same. Somehow, he still hadn't wrapped his head around the fact that he lived here, in the rooms he'd never intended to be anything except possible expansion areas for his business.

He turned over again and stretched. He might as well get up and start the day. Now that he was awake and once again obsessing about the recent past, chances of getting an extra hour of sleep were slim to none.

As the water from the showerhead finished the process of waking him up, Troy cast his mind back to everything that had happened over the past year for what had to be the umpteenth time. Less than a year ago it had all seemed so promising, he mused as he massaged shampoo into his hair. He'd been working in a large and popular tattoo parlor in the center of Dublin but had become more restless by the day. The policies of the place had increasingly eaten away at his love for the job. His creativity had been stifled there and he hadn't been the only one who had felt that way. The memory was as vivid in his mind as if it had happened a week ago. That day he'd been having lunch with Shane, another artist working in the same shop. Shane had spent almost the full hour of their break complaining because their boss had once again vetoed a tattoo he'd designed.

'I've had enough of this fucking shit,' Shane grumbled. 'I want to do my own stuff, not just the pictures in the books or the images Himself comes up with.'

Troy nodded. Designing tattoos wasn't his strong point. He was far better at the actual applying of them, but he recognized Shane's frustration all too well. Himself, also known as their boss, was constantly looking over everybody's shoulder. Giving advice where none was needed, making corrections and suggestions where nothing was wrong. 'What can we do about it? There's no guarantee another parlor wouldn't have the same policies and that's even if they'd take us on. You know how close and incestuous our professional world is. If we leave this job, they might not hire us elsewhere. We'd end up with a reputation as troublemakers.'

'Right.' Shane seemed encouraged rather than disappointed by Troy's words. 'That's why we should start for ourselves. Between your skills with the iron and my drawings, we should have no trouble turning a place of our own into a success.'

At the time, Troy had laughed and refused to take the idea seriously, but a few weeks later, they'd been drawing up plans, making calculations, and before Troy realized exactly what he was doing, they'd resigned from their jobs. *Stupid infatuation.*

He closed his eyes and allowed the water to fall on his head and wash down his body while he wondered whether Shane had always been a dick and he'd just missed the signs, or if the fact that he'd been attracted to Shane had clouded his judgment. One thing he was sure of, though. From now on he'd never allow somebody else to rush him into a decision and he wouldn't be quick to trust or depend on others again, either. There were only two people in the world he would trust from now on—himself and his best friend, Lorcan.

Troy stepped out of the shower, dried himself and threw on some clothes. A long-sleeved T-shirt covered most of the art on his left arm and shoulder. It didn't make sense for a tattoo artist to hide his own tats but the shop got cold during the day and the heating just wasn't up to the job. Yet another thing to worry about considering it was only late October now. He had no idea what he'd do if Ireland experienced a bad winter.

As he sat on the edge of his bed to tie his laces, Troy reflected he should have known something was wrong when Shane had asked him to go and sign the lease on this place on his own. Shane had made a plausible enough excuse at the time, and Troy hadn't been worried when his supposed business partner said he'd add his signature at a later date. *More fool me.* Troy could forgive himself for that first oversight. He'd always tried to see the best in people. It just hadn't been in his nature to be suspicious about people's motives. *I won't be falling into that trap again.* He was far more upset that he'd still refused to see the warning signs when Shane had also left it to him to buy the equipment and furnishings they needed.

Troy stared at the kettle as it heated the water for his first cup of coffee. These thoughts were by now as much part of his morning routine as the shower and caffeine.

Two days before their tattoo parlor was to open, Shane had dropped his bombshell.

'Troy, bud. You won't believe *the opportunity I've been given.' Excitement made Shane's eyes shine.*

'What happened? Well, don't keep me hanging.' It had been hard not to get swept up in Shane's obvious elation.

'I've been chatting with this artist in Florida for months.' Shane grinned widely as the first flicker of unease erupted in Troy's stomach.

'He's so fucking cool, man. Anyway, a while ago I showed him a few of my designs and he loved them.' Shane grinned. 'Fucking deadly, man. He even used one of them.'

'Nice one. Good for you.' Troy hesitated before asking the question he already suspected he didn't want to hear the answer to. 'So, why are you telling me now? Will you be doing more designs

for this man? Is it going to interfere with Pins & Needles?'

Anger coursed through Troy's veins, as if only an hour had passed since the conversation rather than several months. While he poured boiled water on top of the granules in his cup and stirred, he could almost see Shane's guilt-free expression as he'd explained he wouldn't be working with Troy at all, never mind be a partner in their business, because he'd accepted a job offer from the artist in Florida.

He sipped his coffee while listening to the news on the radio and putting some bread in the toaster. Inevitably, Troy's thoughts returned to Shane. None of it would have hurt as much as it did if he hadn't been attracted to Shane. Looking back, Troy realized Shane might well have used that against him. Casual flirtations without ever acting on them had kept Troy fascinated and focused on what might be, rather than the reality. He hated himself for the hope he'd harbored that going into business with Shane might lead to a further mingling of their lives.

Resignation and a dull anger—nothing like the hot fury he'd experienced until recently—coursed through him as he buttered his toast. He still wasn't sure when exactly Shane had started thinking about moving to America. Had Troy and the new parlor only been a back-up plan? Troy hadn't asked. It wouldn't have made a difference either way. The result was the same, whether Shane had planned it that way or not—Troy found himself struggling to run Pins & Needles on his own.

He leaned against the kitchen counter as he ate his toast, studying the space around him. It was a far cry from the much larger, warmer and more modern apartment he used to own. He'd been forced to sell the place once he'd realized he was the sole owner of this business. The money meant he had about a year and a half to make Pins & Needles turn a profit. If he lived frugally, did all the work himself and lived, as he did, in the rooms behind the shop, he would have some time to try to make it work. Of course, having to keep an eye on the pennies meant his social life had dwindled away. He couldn't justify spending money on clubs or overpriced pints in pubs when he needed to make his savings last as long as he possibly could.

"Fuck." His curse bounced off the walls and returned to him. Never mind being disappointed about Shane. He was lonely. He didn't see anybody these days apart from the occasional and way too infrequent customer and his friend, Lorcan. Not that he had time for nights out, and after the Shane fiasco, he wasn't sure he'd ever be able to trust another man again.

After washing his plate and mug, he opened the door connecting his living quarters to the shop and walked over to the counter near the front door. He glanced at the appointment book and saw what he'd known he would see — he had two appointments for today. While he was delighted to have two paying customers, it wasn't enough, especially since both these clients wanted small tattoos. They wouldn't take up a lot of his time and wouldn't bring in any significant money, either. He could only hope they'd leave happy with his work and that word of mouth would lead to more customers.

As he turned to his work station he wished, not for the first time, that he could justify and afford to hire an assistant, even an apprentice. He didn't mind doing all the work himself, but he could do with the distraction, somebody to talk to, somebody who'd take his mind off the memories and worries playing on his mind in a never-ending loop.

Chapter Three

After tossing and turning for an hour, Xander gave up on the hope of falling asleep. He couldn't get his conversation with Eric and the resulting bet off his mind. What had seemed like a great and even fun challenge sixty minutes ago, suddenly felt like a burden. It wasn't that he minded not having sex for a month. He almost welcomed the prospect. He'd been unwilling to admit it, but the flirting, the looks, the pick-up lines and the hurried fucks with men who never lived up to his expectations, had grown old. He still enjoyed the thrill of the chase — except it was rarely a chase these days. His reputation preceded him and whatever flirting did take place was perfunctory, almost a ritual without any of the excitement it used to bring.

Xander half-raised himself, turned over, and punched his pillow into submission, before lying down again. The bet burdened him because it would only be doable if he could find a way to remind himself of the challenge in the heat of the moment. Considering how he invariably detested himself afterward, it was almost funny how he always forgot how much he disliked these casual hook-ups mid-flirt. He never experienced it as boring or repetitive while he stared into the eyes of yet another virtual stranger, or while said stranger fondled his balls and whispered dirty suggestions into his ear. The realization never hit him until the encounter was over, his latest conquest gone again, leaving him with nothing except the memory of a hot but more often than not, forgettable encounter, and yet another set of sheets to wash.

Xander gave up on all hope of sleep, and stared at the

ceiling. Now that he'd accepted Eric's bet he had to come up with a plan. This wasn't the first time he'd decided he needed to slow things down. It was the first time he had another reason, besides his own sanity, to stick to the decision. He sighed. Here he was, twenty-eight years old, with less impulse control than the average teenager. He needed something to remind him to put on the brakes before his horny urges got the upper hand, or he would fall into the same old trap again the next time a handsome face smiled at him.

You can always take your nights out somewhere else. The insecure slut part of his brain wasted no time giving him an out he didn't want. Besides, he had no doubt Eric would consider it cheating if he changed his life around for the duration of the bet. But it was more than that. He needed to change his behavior because he was shredding himself to bits. Every time he hooked up with a man he hoped this time would be different, even if he tried to tell himself he didn't. And without fail those hopes were dashed.

Still restless, Xander got out of bed again and went to the laptop he kept on a small desk in the adjoining room he used as his studio. The screen burst to life when he wiggled the mouse. Without sitting down, he Googled the words *elastic wristband* and stared at the results, then nodded while he read them. He'd been sure he'd heard something about people snapping bands around their wrists to help them with impulse control. The information on his screen confirmed they were used for a whole variety of reasons — to stop swearing, to stay calm, to refrain from over-eating... People turned to them for dealing with anxiety and there was even a link with a title that suggested it could work as an alternative for self-harming.

Xander wouldn't go so far as labeling his sex life a form of self-injury but he couldn't deny his routine had caused him pain, and it hurt more every subsequent time someone walked away. He stared out of the window for a moment as he tried to remember if it had ever been a case of him walking away, or hoping the other man would hurry up and leave already, and sighed when he realized it hadn't happened. No matter how often it had all come to nothing, he'd never really stopped hoping that perhaps the next one...

He turned his gaze back to the screen. If only it were as simple as sticking an elastic band around his wrist. He knew himself well enough to be sure he'd just take the bloody thing off the first time he was tempted by a pretty face or nice arse. He needed something more permanent. Something he wouldn't be able to get rid of easily...or at all. He tried a search for alternatives to elastic wristbands but that only led to links about silicone armbands.

Frustrated he'd come so close to what might have been a solution without actually finding an answer, he closed the laptop again. He glanced over at the nearly finished picture on his drawing board before going over to it. He picked up a pencil and twirled it between his fingers as he studied the image. It didn't need a lot more work. Just a few more details and he'd be ready to add color and bring the project to completion. He frowned. He was fairly certain he'd managed to capture his client's description perfectly but it was impossible to be sure. He'd been making a very successful living from his art for eighteen months now and it still filled him with wonder. He stared at the image and tried to be objective about its qualities, or lack thereof. Technically this was good, even his powerful self-doubt couldn't make him question that. Why people were not only willing to pay large sums of money for his art, but also actively pursued him to accept commissions, was anybody's guess. Surely there were plenty of other artists who could do similar work just as well, and probably cheaper.

He sighed and put the pencil down again. There was no point trying to finish the picture now. He was too restless and filled with doubt to concentrate, and past experience had taught him he'd only mess up a perfectly good piece if he forced the issue. What he needed was a change of scenery. He resolutely turned his back on the unfinished artwork and headed to the bathroom for a shower.

* * * *

An hour, a shower and a breakfast later, Xander put on his coat, picked up his keys and left his apartment. He'd go for a walk to clear his head. It was early and chilly. Bushes were covered in cobwebs. Weak sunlight caught the dew on the spider's threads, giving Xander's urban surroundings a surprisingly magical appearance. His mood lifted as ideas for future projects sprang into his mind. He wandered aimlessly while indulging his artistic ponderings. It wasn't long before the issue that had sent him walking in the first place demanded his attention again.

He didn't pay any attention to his surroundings until, almost two hours later, he noticed the name of the street he was about to turn into. Little Britain Street. As always, the words made him smile, although this morning there was a wry note to it. He'd loved the TV show and still regularly watched reruns of it. On the other hand, today it was all too easy to feel like the 'only gay in town.'

He walked on until a sign he'd never seen before attracted his attention. Pins & Needles it said in bold letters on the window. He'd never seen the tattoo parlor before and wondered if he'd just missed it in the past or whether it was newly opened.

A tattoo is permanent. The idea flashed through his mind and settled there. If he were to get some sort of warning stenciled on his — he considered his options for a moment — hand, he'd have a constant reminder.

He'd taken two steps toward the door when he stopped again. A constant reminder was one thing. A permanent symbol was quite something else. Did he really want to mark himself for life? He tried to imagine what it might be like when a sixty-year-old version of himself glanced at his hand and remembered this moment, and came up blank.

It was just as easy to imagine a tattoo being embarrassing later on in life as it was to assume it might make for a funny story, told years from now.

Frustrated, he turned away. Impulsive as he usually was, he had no doubt he needed to weigh this decision carefully. Tattoos were for life and while he wanted a reminder he couldn't get rid of for the next thirty days, he wasn't sure he'd thank himself if he still had to look at it in a year, never mind ten years from now.

Xander strolled on until he saw a coffee shop. He walked in, ordered a large cappuccino and found himself an empty table. He had to decide whether he was considering this tattoo because he was determined to win the bet or because he really wanted to change the way he lived his life. It would be madness to get a permanent mark on his hand just so he wouldn't lose to Eric, as much as he would hate defeat.

He smiled his thanks at the girl serving him his order, while thoughts continued to race through his head. If he was serious about changing his interactions with men, a fixed reminder wouldn't be a bad idea. And, fuck it, he was serious. It might have taken Eric to open his eyes, but he hadn't been happy for months. He'd known he needed to change his ways for a while now and it wouldn't have taken much longer before his frustration would have gotten the better off him. He wasn't considering this because of the bet and he sure as hell wasn't changing his ways for Eric's sake. If he really wanted a different outcome, he needed a new approach.

He sipped the surprisingly good coffee while he reflected that his love life wasn't the only thing in need of taming. The anger issues he'd had as a teenager had resurfaced lately. He'd come too close to using his fists to vent his frustration and anger in the past few months. So far he'd been able to keep himself in check — well, apart from his assault on the front door earlier that morning — but he'd been tempted to resort to violence instead of words far too often in the recent past. He'd better get a handle on that issue, too, before he found himself in real trouble.

He slowly savored his coffee, while he allowed the idea to play around in his head until he was sure he liked it and probably wouldn't regret it five weeks from now. And—he sat up as the notion struck—if the tattoo worked the way he hoped it would, if he managed to keep himself under control and, who knew, if he did find someone who would be more than a one-night stand, he definitely wouldn't resent the mark in years to come.

Warmth spread through Xander's body as he imagined looking at his hand decades from now with a smile on his face as he remembered how getting the tattoo had been the start of the rest of his life. He almost laughed out loud at himself. Talk about fanciful. Maybe he'd needed Eric to talk to him as if he was a teenage girl in the first throes of lust, he certainly had the dreams to match the picture.

Without giving himself a chance to second-guess his decision again, he got up, walked out of the coffee shop and turned back to the tattoo parlor.

Taking a deep breath, he opened the door and entered. *Rest of my life, here I come.*

Chapter Four

Troy glanced up from the design he was working on when he heard the little bell over his door chime, before looking back down and finishing the last few details. The man who'd entered the shop stopped in front of Troy's counter and cleared his throat.

"Give me a second please." Troy concentrated on the spider he'd drawn—well, copied then embellished on, if he were honest. He wasn't sure why anyone would want a spider on their body—not even a cute and sexy specimen—but that was what the client had asked for and so he'd created one. He tilted his head for a moment before deciding he'd done all he could. Designing tattoos would never be his strong suit but this one wasn't bad at all if he said so himself. The customer who'd asked for the spider would either approve or not, but without feedback, Troy couldn't do anything else.

"Thanks for waiting." Troy straightened and stared at the man on the other side of the counter. He knew him. Or rather, he'd seen him before, Troy was sure of it. The memory he searched for but couldn't put his finger on left a nasty taste in his mouth.

This man had the sort of face that was hard to forget once you'd seen it. Shoulder-length light blond hair stood out against the tan on his face—despite the summer having been over for a few months—giving him a Scandinavian appearance, as did his length and stature. Troy realized he'd been staring and mentally shook himself.

"What can I do for you?"

"Do we know each other?" The man studied Troy with

an intensity that probably mirrored the way Troy had been staring at him only a moment ago, before averting his eyes. "Never mind. I'm thinking about getting a tattoo."

A novice. Troy kept his face straight. This could either be a long and tiresome discussion or great fun, depending on whether or not this was an impulsive walk-in.

"Anything in particular?"

"Yes…" The man hesitated. "Well, no… I mean I've got a fixed idea of what I want it to represent but I'm not sure what it would look like."

"Okay." Troy smiled. "You'll have to be a bit more specific, I'm afraid."

"Yes. Of course."

Troy could have sworn a light blush glowed through the tan on the man's face.

"I want a reminder to take it slow, tattooed on my hand." The man glanced down at his hands on the counter before continuing. "On my right hand to be precise. Because I am right-handed."

The man appeared to be uncertain, as if he was trying to work things out as he talked. Troy stayed silent and waited.

"I considered a stop sign, or something similar, but I don't want anything quite that obvious."

Possible reasons for this request ran through Troy's mind. Was his potential client a smoker trying to quit? An alcoholic staying away from drink? Again the notion that he'd seen this man before hit Troy and he wondered whether he'd understand exactly what the man meant if only he'd be able to place him in the right context. Frustratingly, his memory refused to provide him with the answer.

"What you want is something that will remind you to not do something, without others being able to recognize what it's all about, right?"

The man nodded, clearly relieved he'd been understood.

"So is it something you never want to do again?"

Horror flashed across the man's face before he answered. "No, it's not about abolishing something…" He hesitated.

"I want a reminder to take it slow. I'm not giving anything up."

Probably not drink or smokes then. Troy wasn't sure why he was so curious about what the man wanted to protect himself from. He picked up a sample book from beneath the counter and opened it to the pages with Kanji tattoos.

"How about something like this? These are Japanese designs. We decide on the right message for you. That way only you will be aware of the meaning. Others will only see an intriguing image and it will be up to you whether or not you tell them what it signifies."

The man stared at the pages filled with black characters and studied them before glancing at Troy. "I've no idea what any of these stand for."

Troy laughed. "I'm sorry." He turned the page and revealed the same symbols but this time with the English translations printed underneath. He observed the vaguely familiar man as he studied the characters. It was frustrating. As striking as the customer was, Troy was at a loss to understand why he couldn't place him. When the man tapped a character on the page, Troy diverted his attention back to the sample book.

"That one. Patience. That's the message I want. Right here." The man pointed at the top of his hand, marking out the skin just below his thumb and index finger.

"Off center like that? Are you sure?"

"Yes." The man stared at this hand and nodded. "If we put it there, I'll have the best chance of seeing it when I need the reminder. Why? Isn't it possible to put it there?"

Troy shrugged. "Almost everything is possible. Most people prefer to have their tattoos in places where they can hide them if necessary."

"No." The man appeared to be talking more to himself than to Troy. "Hiding it would defeat the purpose." He looked back up. "When can you do it?"

Troy glanced at his schedule although he had checked it earlier and didn't need to remind himself he'd only one more appointment that day. "It's a small one and only black ink. I could do it later this afternoon, if you're in a hurry. Does four o'clock suit you?"

The man didn't look at his watch or consult a calendar before agreeing.

"I need your name and phone number." Troy picked up a pen.

"Xander Ekman," he answered. "And my number..." Xander fell silent and an expression Troy couldn't name flashed across his face before he rattled the digits off. "I'll be back at four."

Troy kept his gaze on the man — Xander — as he turned away from the counter. As soon as he saw him in profile, Troy remembered exactly and in excruciating detail when he'd seen him before. He opened his mouth to cancel the appointment as Xander reached for the door handle, before closing it again. He couldn't run his business based on personal feelings, no matter how strong or painful. It was obvious his new customer had no idea who Troy was, and why should he? Troy'd gone out of his way to be inconspicuous that night.

As Xander Ekman past the shop window, Troy pushed down the memories trying to unsettle him again. The less time he wasted contemplating things he couldn't change, the better. And since Xander apparently didn't remember him at all, Troy could easily pretend he'd never seen him before. Fate sure was a fickle bitch. Who would have thought that the man who'd, probably unknowingly, crushed Troy's last hope months ago would walk into his parlor?

Chapter Five

Xander didn't think about the possible pain involved in getting a tattoo until he walked back into Pins & Needles almost six hours later.

Reluctant to return home where everything would remind him of yet another one-night stand in a long history of single-night encounters, he'd aimlessly wandered through town. He'd perused the charity shops on Capel Street at his leisure before stopping for lunch in a small restaurant. His window seat had provided him with a view of the Liffey, the river flowing slowly in the middle of the otherwise endless stream of buses, cars and pedestrians making their way into the center of town. Inspired he'd pulled his drawing pad from the backpack he carried and sketched the Ha'penny Bridge, focusing on the young, probably homeless, man sitting with his back against the railing, a cardboard coffee cup in front of him.

When he'd finished eating and his drawing was as good as he could make it with only a black pen, restlessness had him on the pavement again. He made a point of crossing the bridge and dropping all the change he had in his pocket in the young man's cup. It broke his heart when he realized that he'd misjudged the lad's age – he didn't look as if he'd outgrown his teenage years yet. He moved on, thoughts about the beggar and what might have him on the streets replacing his worries about the bet and the tattoo he was about to get in a few hours' time.

When the soles of his feet had started to burn he'd found himself on Parnell Street in front of a cinema with more than two hours left to kill. He'd bought himself a ticket to the latest action blockbuster and, for the first time in his life, entered the theater on his own. The film had served its purpose and taken his mind off both this frustration about his love life — or lack thereof — and the planned tattoo. Even if he'd forgotten what the film had been about fifteen minutes after it ended, it had been worth every cent of the ten Euro he'd spent.

"A punctual customer, it's as rare as it's appreciated."

The man Xander had spoken to earlier smiled at him as he pushed through the door. Xander gave himself a moment to study the artist who would soon inflict pain upon him and give him what he hoped would be the emergency brake he so desperately needed in his life. He was almost as tall as Xander, but where Xander was blond, this man had dark brown hair, cut close to his scalp. He had a smooth, high forehead and pronounced cheekbones. Xander allowed his gaze to linger on the man's mouth for a moment and take in the small ring pierced through the lower of his plump and, right now, smiling lips.

Shit, bollix, fuck. Under any other circumstances he was the kind of man Xander would fall for in about five minutes flat. Why hadn't he seen that before he made the appointment? Xander pushed the thought aside. He was here to get a reminder printed on his hand, and his reaction to the very attractive tattoo artist only reinforced how much he needed it.

"My name is Troy," the man interrupted Xander's thoughts as he stepped from behind the counter with a piece of paper in his hand, which he held out to Xander. "This is what I had in mind for your hand if you still want to go ahead with it."

Xander took the paper and studied the simple yet fascinating image. It resembled a pi sign with a stroke through the left leg and some swirls below it.

"It's small." Xander was torn between relief that whatever getting a tattoo might be like, it probably wouldn't take a long time to create, and disappointment it wouldn't be a bolder statement.

"I can make it bigger" — Troy glanced up from the design and stared at Xander — "but it's going on your hand and I was under the impression this was a personal signal for you rather than a declaration aimed at the rest of the world."

Xander stared from the picture to his hand and back again. The image was about three by three centimeters. He put the paper on the part of his hand where he wanted the tattoo and nodded. It didn't look nearly as small in situ.

"Yes, I see what you mean. This would be great." He took a deep breath before smiling at Troy. "Yes, let's do this."

Troy nodded and turned. "Okay, follow me please."

Xander followed Troy to the back of the store toward an alcove he hadn't noticed before, hidden in the shadows as it was.

"Sit down and try to relax." Troy pointed at the chair, which was a lot like those Xander had seen in dentist offices. The comparison did not make him feel better about what he was about to have done and for the first time since he'd made the appointment, Xander was ambushed by second thoughts.

"So, you've never done this before?" Troy put on surgical gloves before wiping Xander's hand with what smelled like an antiseptic substance. "There's no artwork hidden under your clothes?"

What should have been an innocent question stirred something in Xander and his cock twitched in his pants. His second thoughts vanished. If he'd had any doubt about whether or not he needed this tattoo, his body had just given him a much needed reminder why he was about to get a symbol etched on his hand.

"No. No tattoos or piercings anywhere. In fact, before today, I never even played with the idea of getting a tattoo."

"Oh." Troy stepped back, a frown forming on his forehead. "In that case, we should probably wait a while. You need to take a few days and make sure this is really what you want. A tattoo is not easy to get rid of once you're inked. It's not something to do on the spur of the moment."

"No!" Xander didn't realize he'd raised his voice until Troy arched one eyebrow at him. "I mean, I did think about it. It has more or less been the only thing on my mind for the past six hours. This is what I want." *And what I need.* Xander had no intention of sharing that urgency with Troy and could only hope his tone of voice hadn't betrayed the emotion.

It was hard not to squirm or look away as Troy stared at him, apparently trying to make up his mind about whether or not Xander really knew what he wanted. A flash of anger ran through Xander. This wasn't the only place in town if he wanted a tattoo. If Troy refused to do it he'd go somewhere else. In fact, he'd just go. He didn't need this. He was twenty-eight years old, for God's sake, more than old enough to make decisions for himself. He opened his mouth to say as much.

"Okay, as long as you're sure." Troy's face had gone blank, but Xander couldn't shrug off the idea that Troy had left the words *'it's your funeral'* unspoken at the end of his sentence. He resumed cleaning Xander's hand before pressing the paper with the design down to his skin, just to the right of his thumb.

Suddenly nervous again, Xander watched as Troy rubbed over the paper before lifting it. The image had transferred from the paper to his hand and Xander stared at it in wonder. It was perfect. The size was just right, the image exactly in the spot he'd had in mind and he could imagine catching a glimpse of it the next time he was about to act on impulse and needed the reminder.

"Is that okay for you?" Troy asked.

"Yes." Xander smiled. "It looks even better than I hoped it would."

"Good." Troy turned to the trolley next to the chair and Xander watched as he poured black ink into a small cup. When Troy picked up what could only be described as an intricate gun, Xander swallowed hard while his mouth went dry and his heartbeat sped up.

"How much is this going to hurt?" Despite trying to sound matter-of-fact, Xander could hear the note of uncertainty in his own voice.

"That's hard to predict. Apart from anything else it depends a lot on your personal pain threshold." Doubt stared at Xander from Troy's eyes. "We really don't have to do this now. You could go home and come back after the weekend."

This time the suggestion almost tempted Xander before he caught himself. "No. I really prefer to get it done and over with now. I was just curious, since this is a first for me." Xander didn't trust himself to come back if he walked away now. Besides, the weekend was upon him, which meant he'd probably need the reminder sooner rather than later. If he didn't do this today he probably never would, which in turn would mean he'd almost certainly lose his bet and, if he were honest, what little self-respect he had left. It was going to stop here and now, regardless of the pain involved.

"Well," Troy said, "I wouldn't have advised starting with a tattoo on your hand. It hurts less on areas with a lot of fat or muscle." Troy rubbed a finger over the transfer on Xander's hand and the surprisingly intimate contact sent a shiver down Xander's spine.

"On the other hand," Troy continued, "most of this image is situated over a part of your hand with no bones beneath the skin so it shouldn't be as bad as it could be. At least you're starting off small."

"What do you mean?"

"You'd be surprised how" — Troy seemed to search for the right word —"over confident some people are. They come in here, newbies like you, and insist they want something huge, like a full sleeve."

"Full sleeve?" Xander had no idea what Troy was talking about and watched in fascination as Troy pushed the sleeve of his shirt up to reveal an arm filled with swirls of colors and intricate patterns.

"Full sleeve. It goes from the wrist to the shoulder," Troy said.

Xander stared at the design and just for a moment allowed himself to imagine tracing his finger along those lines.

"And there's nothing wrong with that in and of itself, but it's not uncommon for them to have completely underestimated the amount of time it takes or the pain involved. I make a point of creating those tattoos in carefully designed portions so they don't end up looking like complete fools if they decide they want to stop after one or two sessions." Troy picked up the gun as he continued, "So, yeah, small is good. This should be all done in about an hour."

Some of Xander's apprehension left him again. An hour was doable, provided it didn't hurt too much. He'd be fine. He needed to do this. He could take sixty minutes of discomfort or pain to make it happen.

Chapter Six

Troy turned his machine on, still not entirely sure he shouldn't just send Xander away to sleep on his decision. He'd done it in the past and he'd lost one or two customers that way. Customers he could ill afford to lose. But Xander seemed sure of what he wanted and determined to get it done today, and since he was a grown man, who was Troy to argue?

"The more you relax, the easier it will be." Troy said the words, as he always did, despite knowing that just mentioning the need to relax was usually enough to make people tense up. His wish for two sets of eyes was nothing new, either. It would be so much easier if he could keep an eye on Xander's face as well as the work he was doing on his hand. But he couldn't and concentrating on the design took precedence, so he did the next best thing and listened to Xander's breathing which was just about audible over the humming of the machine.

"Are you okay?" Troy paused for a moment in reaction to Xander's quick intake of breath.

"Yeah." Xander sounded slightly breathless but determined. "It's not too bad I guess."

Thoughts flowed through Troy's mind as he concentrated on his work. He'd love to discover what this design meant to Xander. Why did he need patience visible on his hand? What was the man impatient about, and why was his need to fight the impulse so strong he'd turned to a tattoo? The question burned on his lips but he refrained from asking it. Experience had taught him that customers talked about their reasons for picking a particular design unless they really wanted to keep them private. Asking was either unnecessary or useless so he didn't. In fact, most customers were more talkative than Xander was right now. If it wasn't for the fact that Xander didn't move his hand at all and seemed to have his breathing under control again, Troy would have worried about his silence. Troy could have done with the distraction of a conversation, though, as memories of the only other time he'd ever seen this man worked their way to the forefront of his mind.

"So, how do I take care of that hand after I leave here?" Xander asked.

Troy smiled to himself. Just when he'd been getting worried about the man not talking he opened his mouth. What's more, he might have misjudged him. If Xander had forethought enough to ask about aftercare before Troy mentioned it, he was approaching this decision with more consideration than Troy had given him credit for. And, of course, giving practical advice meant he didn't have time to linger on the images flickering through his mind.

"I'll bandage it before you leave. It needs to be covered for twenty-four hours but you'll want to change the dressing a few times to prevent it from sticking to what will effectively be a wound for a while."

"And after that first day? Does it take long to heal completely?"

Troy had finished the outline and took a moment to glance at his customer. "You should probably have asked those questions before we started. What if you don't like the answers?"

"Nah, the answers wouldn't have made a difference. I *need* this tattoo." Xander stopped talking and looked away, leaving Troy to wonder again why on earth this small tattoo was so very important to him.

"I'll give you a leaflet with all the information before you go," Troy said. "It's simple enough and basically boils down to being careful and hygienic." Troy glanced at the half-finished tattoo on Xander's hand. "The next part will hurt a bit more, filling in always does."

"Okay." Xander also stared at his right hand but averted his gaze as soon as Troy reapplied the machine. He worked in silence and it wasn't long before he was done.

"There. Is that what you had in mind?"

"It's perfect. Thank you."

Troy watched closely as a range of emotions flitted across his client's face. He recognized surprise, followed by delight and finally something like a mixture of pride and regret. Troy mentally shook himself. He was getting fanciful. A mixture of pride and regret, *indeed*. If he'd been alone he would have snorted out loud. He didn't know this man well enough to recognize emotions like that. In fact, Xander was a complete stranger, even if he had seen him before under circumstances he'd rather forget. And wouldn't mind seeing him again. *Where the fuck had that* thought *come from*?

Troy went through the routine of cleaning the tattooed area and applying the covering. "That's you done. Just take care of it as it says in the leaflet. If you are worried about it at any stage, come back and I'll take a look. The only thing you need to be on the lookout for is an infection." Troy saw the worried expression on Xander's face and went on, "Infection really only happens to those who don't treat the new tattoo correctly, so it shouldn't be an issue, right?"

"Yes." Xander smiled, which brought his handsome face close to beautiful. "Don't worry about me treating it right. I'm a bit of a wimp so I'm not taking any risks."

"I'm glad to hear it." Troy couldn't help but return the smile before he turned away from the chair and started toward to the counter in the front part of the shop. He heard rather than saw Xander get up and follow him.

"Shit." Xander had his left arm awkwardly wrapped around his back. "Should have thought of that." He mumbled the words but Troy could hear them clearly enough.

"What's wrong?"

"Hmmm? Nothing. I should have put my wallet in my other pocket before we did this. Who knew it would be this hard to get something out of my right-side back pocket with my left hand?"

"Come here to me, let me help you," Troy rounded the counter and chuckled softly as he extracted the offending item and handed it to Xander, noting the slight blush on his customer's face with interest. He took the offered credit card and bit back a smile when Xander made a point of putting the wallet in his left pocket after the transaction had been finalized.

"That's gonna take some getting used to." Xander shook his head and smiled.

"And just when you are used to it you'll be able to use your right hand again." Troy mirrored Xander's smile and he wondered what was wrong with him. Handsome as Xander was, Troy wasn't in the habit of flirting with his customers and with this particular client he had more than one reason to keep his distance.

As Xander turned to leave, Troy couldn't stop himself from opening his mouth. "Remember, if you're worried at all just come back and I'll take a look."

"Sure. Thanks."

When his phone rang, Troy realized he'd been staring at the door through which Xander had left. He snorted at himself. It had been a while since a man had made so much of an impression on him in such a short time. He glanced at the screen before answering.

"Lorcan. Wait till I tell you who just walked out of my shop."

"Hello to you, too," Lorcan said, chuckling. "Well, don't leave me hanging, who just left?"

"Do you remember Shane's going-away party?" Troy didn't wait for an answer but rushed on, "The man Shane picked up that night showed up for a tattoo today."

"And?" Lorcan asked. "Did you two talk about your erstwhile business partner?"

"God, no." The idea horrified Troy. "I didn't even tell him I'd seen him before. Last thing I need is somebody gushing about how wonderful Shane is."

"True," Lorcan said. "In fact, you could do with spending less time obsessing about that man. He's out of your life now, and good riddance, if you ask me. In fact, I may just have the perfect distraction for you."

"Okay, tell me more."

"Guess who managed to get his hands on tickets for that exhibition you were talking about the other day?" Lorcan sounded smug and Troy could imagine the satisfied expression on his friend's face all too well.

"The local artists' showcase? You have tickets for the opening night? Where did you get those? They're like fucking gold dust."

"My boss got them but he and his wife can't go. He asked if I would be interested and I remembered what you said about it a week ago and jumped on the opportunity. I take it you're available to go with me on Monday night?"

"Abso-fucking-lutely." Troy couldn't believe his luck. "That means I'll be able to talk to those artists without having to approach them individually. Who knows, I may find someone who'd be interested in occasionally drawing a design for me at some point in the future." *When I can afford to pay them.* He didn't add those words. "Lorcan, you're the best."

"Yeah, yeah. I know you love me." The humor in Lorcan's voice made Troy laugh.

"Okay, mate, I've gotta go. I'll drop by tomorrow night with Chinese. We can make arrangements then."

Troy relaxed, something he rarely did these days. Now he had both their already planned Saturday night get-together and the exhibition on Monday to look forward to. It didn't make for a social life, but it sure beat his normal, solitary nights watching mindless television. "Great. See you then. Have a good one." Troy ended the call and, for the first time since he'd opened his shop, dared to hope that his luck might be changing.

Chapter Seven

"What'd you do to your hand?"

Eric walked in and asked the question only minutes after Xander had returned home and collapsed on the couch. Of course Eric had noticed the dressing instantly and jumped on it like a hungry dog on a bowl of food. Xander had known he wouldn't be able to hide either the bandage now or the tattoo after tomorrow from his friend, but he wouldn't have minded a bit more time to decide what he wanted to say about it. He didn't want to lie to Eric. He never had in the past and after eighteen years of being best friends, he'd no intention of starting now. On the other hand, now that he had the tattoo he felt a bit foolish about the whole thing. Needing a tattoo to remind himself to behave didn't show a lot of faith in his powers of self-control.

Damn it. If I can't tell Eric the truth, who can I talk to? "I went and got a tattoo."

"You did what? Since when are you interested in tattoos?" Eric's surprise made Xander smile.

"Since today. I saw the shop and had this idea and in the spirit of there's no time like the present I got the tattoo set there and then."

Eric stared at Xander for a few moments as if he wanted to figure out whether or not his friend had lost his mind at last. "You do realize those things are permanent, right? It's the sort of decision most people sit on for a while, sleep on even."

"Yeah, yeah" — Xander waved his left hand through the air — "I know. The tattoo artist said pretty much the same thing and even told me I should probably wait until after the weekend."

"Well, I guess that's something," Eric said. "And you didn't take his advice because…?"

"I wasn't going to change my mind and I needed to have it done now." Xander silently cursed himself for having used the word *need*, while hoping that Eric wouldn't pick up on it.

"You needed to get a tattoo today? You never considered getting one and then the moment the idea popped into your head you decided that it couldn't possibly wait until after the weekend?"

"Something like that," Xander muttered the words, hoping against hope Eric would drop the subject.

As he'd known would be the case, Xander's reply roused Eric's curiosity enough for him to change his normal coming home routine. He didn't go to his own room first to change into more comfortable clothes but instead sat down on the couch, in the far corner from where Xander sat. "Shoot."

"Hey, since when do I have to explain all my actions to you? You're not my parent and I'm grown-up, as in old enough to make my own decisions for my own reasons," Xander nearly growled his reply.

"Touchy much?" Eric tilted his head, entirely unimpressed by Xander's tone of voice and choice of words. "Now I'm really curious. Spill. You know you will eventually."

Xander sighed. "Seriously? Can we just let it be? I wanted a tattoo. I got one. Big deal."

"What did you get anyway?"

Xander glared at his friend. It wasn't like Eric to stop pushing so easily.

"It's a Japanese character."

"Show me."

"I can't. I'm supposed to keep it covered for twenty-four hours." Xander didn't see any reason why he should mention that he was supposed to change the bandage at least once during that same time period.

Eric picked up a notepad and pencil from the coffee table

and threw them at Xander. "Draw it for me."

Xander sank back against the pillows on the couch while he silently admitted defeat. He could have saved his breath since he'd known he'd find himself telling Eric about the tattoo and why he'd gotten it sooner rather than later. One glance at Eric and the rapt expression on his face told Xander the game was up and with a sigh he drew out the character from memory before handing the notebook back.

Eric looked at the image for a few moments before turning to Xander. "So, what does it mean? There is a translation right? This stands for something."

For half a second Xander played with the idea of not telling Eric what the symbol meant, before realizing Eric could just Google it.

"It's the Japanese character for patience."

Eric sank back against the pillows and studied Xander. "Patience? Please tell me you didn't...."

Xander concentrated on the dressing on his hand and said nothing.

"Dude, it seems to me you're taking this bet a bit too seriously."

Damn the man. Sometimes it sucked having a friend who knew you inside out and had some special talent when it came to reading people's expressions. Unprepared to explain all his reasons to Eric and unable to come up with another plausible reason for the choice, Xander said nothing and continued to look anywhere except at Eric.

"Don't you think that's a rather permanent solution for what was always going to be a temporary issue?" Eric asked, no longer joking or light-hearted. "The bet was supposed to be a bit of fun. A challenge for you. Something we could laugh about. Jaysus, if I'd known you were going to take it this seriously I wouldn't have suggested it."

Just like that, Xander felt like shit. He didn't want Eric blaming himself for something that wasn't his fault. It was time to act like the adult he purported to be and answer the man's questions. Didn't mean he had to like it though.

"It's not just the bet." Xander worked hard to keep his voice neutral and avoided looking at Eric. Of course, after knowing him for almost two decades, Xander didn't need to see Eric to predict what expression he'd have on his face right now. He could imagine the slightly tilted head and the question in Eric's eyes with such clarity, he might as well be looking at him.

"What was it then?" Eric's voice was soft.

Xander fought with himself. He didn't want to spell it out for Eric. It had been hard enough to admit to himself that he wasn't strong enough to keep himself under control. He really didn't want to say it out loud too. On the other hand, if he admitted that he wanted more than just a month worth of abstinence, that he was fed up with the way he'd been conducting his love life, he might get some support along the way. But he'd leave it at that. No way was he mentioning the anger issue, as well. Eric wasn't aware that Xander's teenage problem had resurfaced in the recent past, and that suited Xander just fine.

"After we talked last night..." Xander peeked at Eric through his eyelashes and saw what he'd expected to see – his friend's undivided attention. "I couldn't sleep. I thought about the bet and a month without hooking up with anyone and all I experienced was relief. And I decided that yes, I did want to win the bet but more than that, I wanted to stop picking up men left, right and center completely, not just for a month."

"That's great. You never used to..." Eric trailed off, as if he was lost for words.

"I never used to whore around like that?" Xander aimed for light-hearted and funny but clearly heard the bitter tone in his own voice.

"I wouldn't put it quite like that." Eric sounded very matter of fact. "It's not like your behavior is exceptional and compared to some, your sex life is positively boring. That's not why I brought it up and you know it. This isn't you. You weren't like this when I left for Canada. You weren't even this eager when you were a hormonal teenager. I mentioned it because I'm not convinced it makes you happy."

"It does while I'm in the thick of it." Xander muttered. "I got fed up with relationships that really weren't relationships at all. Out of all the men I hooked up with only two stayed in touch after that first night, and that was only for sex, too. And then they got bored after a few weeks, tops. I figured if men weren't going to stick around anyway, there was no point putting all that energy into getting to know them and trying to ease them into my life. I convinced myself hooking up for sex without commitments was easier. And for a while it was." Xander shrugged. "It isn't anymore. In fact, it's rather unsatisfying" — he frowned — "well, except for the moment when I'm actually coming."

"So what are you saying?" Eric's scrutiny was growing ever more uncomfortable.

"I'm not sure." Xander recognized the disbelief on Eric's face. "I really don't. I know I don't want to continue what I was doing." He shrugged. "I guess the tattoo is a reminder that nothing needs to happen right here and now, that there's no harm waiting another day or week or however long."

"Halle-fucking-lujah." A grin stretched across Eric's face. "That sounds like the Xander I grew up with." His smile widened. "If you'd said that yesterday I would never have suggested the bet. We could call it off, if you want. Seems the goal has been achieved in less than a day."

Xander opened his mouth to agree but one glance at his hand made him close it again and he took a moment to consider the suggestion. "No. Let's keep the bet going. Unless you want out now that I've made sure your chances of winning are zero." Xander raised his eyebrow.

"No, you're good." Eric relaxed into the cushions on the couch and winked. "This is one bet I don't mind losing. And you still have twenty-nine days to go. Let's see how determined you are once some time has passed and you have a few drinks inside you."

That's what the tattoo is for. Xander didn't say the words out loud while he softly rubbed the bandage. A weight had been lifted off his shoulders. He wasn't one for talking about his emotions with his friends but he couldn't deny that sharing some of his thoughts with Eric had helped. Such a shame he and Eric had never been attracted to each other. What Xander needed in his life was a man who understood him the way Eric did, not just as a friend but as his partner. He didn't fancy his chances of ever running into that man.

Chapter Eight

Troy breathed a sigh of relief as he turned the sign from *open* to *closed*. He was exhausted. He locked the door and entered his living quarters. For once it was the good kind of tired though. This Saturday had gone surprisingly well. When he'd opened Pins & Needles he'd only had one appointment in his book. He'd mentally prepared himself for another long and probably boring day, only to find himself rushed off his feet and barely able to keep up with the inquiries from all the people who'd come through his door. To end the day with six new bookings, as well as a possible one — provided he could work out the details — was more than he could have hoped for. He'd also had two walk-ins for small tattoos. If more days were like today he might be able to convince himself he stood a chance of making this business work.

He threw a glance in the direction of his couch, noticing, not for the first time, that the piece of furniture was too big for the room it was in, before going to his bedroom and shedding his clothes. He had about thirty minutes before Lorcan was due to arrive with a take-away meal for them. He desperately needed a shower. In an ideal world, the wash would have been followed by a nap on his too big but oh-so-comfortable couch, but his last unscheduled customer had kept him busy longer than expected, so a lie-down wasn't on the cards.

Still, he mused as he turned on the water, as complaints went, this was a good one. While being kept going continuously throughout the day had been a shock to the system, it was also exactly what he needed if he wanted

Pins &Needles to survive.

After a quick wash, he closed his eyes and turned the temperature of the water up a notch, grateful he'd allowed himself the indulgence of an electric shower. As the water fell on his head and shoulders Troy allowed the heat to relax his muscles. Tension slowly left his body and when he stepped out of the shower, fifteen minutes after starting it, he felt almost as good as new.

He'd only dried and dressed himself when he heard a knock on the shop door. He checked the time and discovered that his friend was ten minutes early. Then again, Lorcan was never late and never unprepared. As frustrating as Lorcan's need to always get every detail right could be, Troy couldn't deny it was satisfying to have a friend he could trust and depend upon without doubt or question.

When Troy opened the door, a gust of wind blew cold rain in his face. Lorcan pushed him out of the way as he all but ran in, scowling at Troy as he went.

"You took your bloody time."

Troy bit the inside of his cheek to stop himself from laughing out loud. His life-long friend looked like a drowned puppy. Lorcan's shaggy hair, normally kept in place with a liberal dosing of gel, had collapsed under the onslaught of water and lay flat on his head, tiny droplets falling to his already drenched shoulders. His trousers were soaked and clung to his muscular legs. The resulting image wouldn't have been remarkable on most men, but Lorcan almost never wore tight clothes so it was a sight Troy wasn't used to.

When the urge to laugh had passed, Troy turned away from the door and waved at Lorcan to get him moving. "Go on through. Take a shower if you need to get warm again and take those clothes off. You can borrow a pair of jogging pants and a hoody for the time being."

Troy followed Lorcan as his friend dripped his way through the shop and into the back rooms.

"Bloody weather," Lorcan growled as he dropped the

plastic bag he'd been carrying on the coffee table before heading to Troy's bedroom, already fumbling with the button on his trousers. "It was dry with clear skies when I left the house."

"I know," Troy replied. "It was dry when I locked up the shop, too. I'd no idea it had started to rain." He walked to his chest of drawers and pulled out a few items of clothing before laying them on the bed next to where Lorcan stood. He passed a towel to the now all but naked Lorcan and watched as the man hastily yet thoroughly dried himself.

Not for the first time Troy wondered what life would have been like if he and Lorcan had just fallen for each other. After all, they'd been as thick as thieves from the moment they'd started school, at age five. He smiled ruefully as he remembered how his father had reacted when he came out, ten years ago now. He could still hear the old man's voice in his head.

'I knew it. It's that Lorcan fellow, isn't it? He's filled your head with these weird ideas, hasn't he?'

At the time the statement had come as a huge shock. Close as they'd been, Lorcan and Troy had never come out to each other. Until his father had mentioned it, Troy hadn't even considered that Lorcan might be gay too.

"Troy?"

"Hmmm?" Troy was surprised to discover that Lorcan had managed to get fully dressed while he'd been lost in his memories.

"I said" — Lorcan gave him a quizzical look — "that we should probably eat now unless you want to reheat it all later."

"God, no. We're eating now. I'm starving." Troy turned on his heel and marched to the kitchen where he collected plates and cutlery. When he walked into the living room, Lorcan had pulled the containers from the bag and placed them on the table, lids removed. Troy stared at the amount of food in front of him in wonder.

"Did you invite others to join us?" He knew perfectly well

Lorcan would never do such a thing without talking to him first, but there was no way the two of them could even make a dent in everything that was on offer, never mind finish it.

"Nah. Couldn't make up my mind what I wanted. So I guess I went over the top and just picked all our favorites." Lorcan smirked at the spread on the coffee table. "Turns out, we've got quite few of those."

Lorcan took the plate Troy held out to him and filled it with small portions from every single dish. Troy shrugged and copied Lorcan's actions. The food would get eaten, if not today then over the next few days.

"Tell me, what had you so distracted just now?" Lorcan asked once they'd settled on the couch, plates on their laps.

Troy swallowed, his mouth full of chicken in black bean sauce, before answering. "I remembered the day my father outed you to me."

"Jaysus. Don't remind me." Lorcan appeared almost as horrified as he had the day Troy had just asked him straight out whether or not he was gay. "I'm still not sure I would have come out at all if it hadn't been for your da."

"What?" Troy put his fork down and turned to study the man he'd thought he knew very well. "Not at all? What were you going to do instead? Get married to a girl?"

An expression of mild disgust swept across Lorcan's face before his features relaxed into a rueful smile. "No. I figured I could easily be one of those eternal bachelors. I mean, not everybody hooks up or gets married."

"Do I even know you?" Troy was gobsmacked. True, they'd never talked in so many words about how they saw their individual futures, but Troy had always assumed that Lorcan's hopes and dreams were more or less the same as his. And Troy most definitely saw himself in a lasting and stable relationship at some point in the future.

"Don't turn it into a bigger deal than it is." Lorcan seemed almost irritated. "I'm just not convinced I'm built for relationships. You are about the only person in my life who doesn't get on my nerves after a few hours. And the idea of having to share my personal space with somebody else all the time…" He grimaced. "Let's just say I'm far too comfortable in my own company."

"Wow. Color me shocked." Troy shook his head and redirected his attention to the food on his plate while he processed what he'd just heard. He wasn't sure whether he was jealous because Lorcan had turned being happy on his own into an art form, or pitied his friend because he'd more or less condemned himself to a lonely life.

Lorcan stood and refilled his plate. "Anyway, enough about me. How was your day? You sounded rushed when I called you. Aren't you supposed to be closed between one and two?"

"I didn't close for lunch today. A grin spread across Troy's face. I didn't have the time."

"That's fantastic." Lorcan smiled back at him. "A busy day, then?"

"The very first day of back-to-back customers." Troy still couldn't get over the wonder of it. Until this morning, he'd been convinced he'd never see more than a sporadic customer walk through his door. He realized today could easily have been a fluke, but in the back of his mind, buried under all the stress and worry, a tiny flicker of hope had sprung to life. If he experienced a few more days like the one he'd had, he might be able to convince himself that he *could* make this work. "At least a few of them only came in for a consult and quote, and one of them I'll probably have to refer to another parlor. But" — he still couldn't quite believe it — "by the end of the day I had six new bookings and two small tattoos set."

"Why won't you be able to take on that one customer?" Lorcan asked between bites of food.

"He gave me an elaborate description of the image he has in mind. It is not like anything I've seen before and although I can clearly conjure up what he means in my mind, I'm nowhere near good enough to draw it for him."

"Isn't that one of the reasons you want to go to that

exhibition?" Lorcan asked. "To meet artists and see if one or more of them might be interested in drawing for you?"

"Yeah." Troy placed his plate on the table, no longer hungry. "But it's too soon. The way things are, there's no way I can afford to pay an artist for original designs. Have you seen the prices their pieces fetch?" He didn't realize he'd been frowning until Lorcan reached over and squeezed his shoulder.

"I know," Lorcan said. "And if Shane hadn't been such a dick and had kept his word and become your business partner, you wouldn't be in this position."

A dart of anger so fresh it shocked him shot through Troy. He'd obviously not dealt with his Shane issues as well as he'd hoped. Sure, the man and his betrayal still played on his mind a lot, but he hadn't realized how close to the surface the emotions still were. Clearly he was nowhere near over the whole experience, or perhaps all the memories that man, Xander had triggered had set him back. It really didn't matter where the depth of his anger came from because it didn't change the fact that Shane would have been able to create the image his customer had described this afternoon. Shane might be a royal bastard, but that didn't make him any less good at what he did.

He took a deep breath. None of this was Lorcan's fault. In fact, Lorcan had tried to discourage him when he'd first mentioned the idea of going into business with Shane. Lorcan's instincts had been right, his advice good, but Troy had called him overly cautious and brushed his suggestions off.

"But the show on Monday will hopefully help in the long-term." He put as much joviality in his voice as he could muster. "Even if I can't hire artists now, that doesn't mean I can't introduce myself to them, get acquainted with their work and find out if they'd be interested in commissions from me in the future."

Lorcan turned to face him, a wide smile Troy didn't understand stretched across his face.

"What?"

"Did you listen to yourself?" Lorcan asked, beaming at Troy. "This is the first time since you've opened the shop that you've allowed yourself to talk about the future as if you actually believe you can make this business work."

Troy was taken aback. Had he really been that negative about his prospects in the past? He didn't need to linger on that question for very long before he realized he'd never even allowed himself to dream it might work, never mind count on it. Which led to the question whether or not he really was more hopeful now.

"One good day doesn't make for a successful business." He stopped and pondered where his earlier burst of optimism had come from.

"True," Lorcan said. "Remember, I'm an accountant. I see way too many business owners with dismal sales figures having the exact opposite attitude to yours. They're so determinedly optimistic they fail to recognize their business is collapsing around their ears. That's why I'm convinced you've got a real chance of making it."

"Say what?" Troy stared at Lorcan, trying to figure out what his friend might mean.

"The way I see it" — Lorcan placed his plate on the table and settled back against the couch cushions, making himself comfortable — "a positive mindset is what you need, not blind optimism. You don't want to be so over-confident that you start making expenses and investments you can't afford. On the other hand, you also want to avoid being so careful that you allow opportunities to pass you by. You need to find a balance."

"Sure" — Troy was still confused — "but how does that apply to me?"

"Well, look at your situation. A blind optimist would still be living in his old apartment, having to pay for a mortgage as well as the lease here, confident that he'd eventually be successful enough to pay off all the overdrafts that would require. You on the other hand did the sensible thing, sold your apartment and moved in here so that you now have some money to tie you over until the business does sustain itself and you."

Troy frowned and Lorcan laughed.

"I realize living here is far from ideal. But, more days like today, more clients and hopefully more word of mouth, and your reputation will grow and so will your business. If that happens before you run out of your reserve funds – and I don't see any reason why it shouldn't – you will have built yourself a solid foundation for future success. The trick is to find the right balance between investment and restraint and it seems to me you've struck that pretty well."

"Hmmm," Troy was lost for words. He liked the sound of Lorcan's perspective and he couldn't deny his friend was an expert when it came to finances, but that didn't mean Troy could share his optimism. Sure, he was delighted with how today had worked out but surely it was way too early to draw any conclusions from it. He said as much and Lorcan nodded.

"Yes, you're right. One good day does not make your shop a success. But you have to start somewhere and a negative attitude is definitely not going to help. So why not try to enjoy the unexpected good news, while keeping an open mind about the future?"

"Fair enough." For the first time since he'd started out on his own Troy didn't feel as if he was carrying the weight of the world on his shoulders. "I can do open minded. Just don't ask me to start celebrating yet."

"I won't. Instead I'll ask you to turn that box on and start *Destiny*. One of these days I'll beat you at the bloody game."

Chapter Nine

"Here you go." Eric put a pint of Guinness in front of Xander and sat on a stool on the other side of the high, round table.

"Thanks. *Slainté*." Xander took a long sip of his drink while glancing around the bar. The place was busy but not packed. No doubt that would change over the next few hours but for now it was still possible to have a conversation without having to shout.

He'd been tempted to stay at home tonight, but Eric had insisted he needed a change of scenery and didn't want to go out on his own. It hadn't seemed fair on his friend to refuse just because Xander had felt somewhat insecure ever since he'd gotten his tattoo. *How fucked-up was that?* The tattoo was supposed to give him some much-needed support, not make him even less confident than he'd been before he got it.

He rubbed the thumb of his left hand over the bandage he'd decided to keep on for longer than was strictly necessary. According to the instructions he could have taken it off by now, but for reasons he couldn't quite explain to himself he'd put a fresh one over the image before going out, hiding it rather than leaving it uncovered.

"I'm still in shock about that tattoo of yours," Eric stated.

Xander snickered. "So am I."

"You regret it now?" Eric sounded mildly worried.

"No, I don't regret it." Xander shrugged. "I'm just surprised I jumped into it with so little forethought." He saw Eric open his mouth to interrupt him and hurried on. "I mean I did think about all the pros and cons. And there

54

were several hours between talking to the artist and getting the thing set, so it wasn't completely spur of the moment, but still, I've taken longer to make up my mind about which color to paint my walls than I did this decision."

"Maybe you should have taken the tattoo's meaning — you know, patience— into consideration before actually getting it," Eric suggested with a wink.

"Very funny," Xander replied while silently conceding that Eric might have made a valid point. "Anyway, it's done now. It's small and it is an interesting character, which most people won't even understand." *And a reminder I could really use in my life.* Xander kept that sentiment to himself.

"So, tell me something." Xander decided to take the conversation away from his tattoo, if not the reason for getting it. "What was it like for you in Canada? Am I to believe you were celibate while you were there?"

"God, no! What do you take me for? A monk?" Eric threw his head back and laughed. "I was there for two years, remember?"

"Well then" —Xander was truly curious—"what's with your obsession with my love life? Clearly you didn't pick up your life-long partner in Canada either, so how are your hook-ups different from mine?"

Eric stopped laughing and stared at Xander for long enough to make him wonder whether he'd gone too far. What if Eric's coming back to Ireland had meant leaving somebody important behind? Eric had never said and Xander had never inquired.

"Sorry. Forget I asked that. It's none of my business." Xander looked around the pub in the faint hope of recognizing someone who might come over and interrupt this now rather uncomfortable conversation.

"No, it's okay. I guess it's a fair question considering how I stuck my nose into your private life." Eric was quiet for a few moments while he stared off into the distance. "I had two short-lived relationships while I was in Toronto." He'd turned back to Xander with a relaxed but somewhat wistful expression on his face. "Both times I knew they wouldn't be long-term commitments before they even started. Those men were nice, attractive and good company. I enjoyed spending time with them and sure, we had our fair share of fun in the bedroom…and most other rooms." Eric winked. "But it was all based on nothing more and nothing less than mutual attraction and availability." He stared at his pint for a moment before adding, "Which was, of course, just as well since I was never going to stay there."

As Xander listened he became aware of an emotion he could only describe as jealousy creeping up on him. If he'd been able to hook up with men who were interested in a relationship like the one Eric had just described, he wouldn't be in the predicament he now found himself in.

"But," Eric continued, oblivious to Xander's inner turmoil, "the whole thing developed like you'd expect a relationship to develop. You know, meeting someone, going for a drink or a bite to eat, and taking things further once we'd established that we did indeed like each other. It's been years since my last one-night stand."

Xander tried to imagine it— meeting an attractive guy in a bar like the one they were in and just chatting before arranging to meet again at a later date—and couldn't see it happening. Most men here tonight had come in the hope of picking someone up before the evening was over. The ones who hadn't, had probably arrived with either a friend or a steady partner. Eric's experiences sounded like something you'd read about in a romance novel. Where was he supposed to meet these men he'd go on a date with if not in a gay bar or club? And if he met them here, it was almost expected that he'd have some sort of sexual experience with them before morning. An idea struck him and he smiled ruefully.

"What's with the smirk?" Eric asked.

"It just occurred to me that perhaps we should have set the embargo for longer than one month."

"Why do you say that?"

"Because" — Xander took a deep breath — "I clearly need to figure out a new way of approaching this finding a man thing, and that may not be as easy as it sounds."

An emotion close to frustration crossed Eric's face. "Now you're just being over-dramatic. I'm talking about delayed gratification, not rocket science." He softened his tone. "So those men in the past have disappointed you and now you've convinced yourself every single man you're going to meet is going to be the same?"

Eric's question sounded reasonable in theory. If only Xander's reality over the past eighteen months or so wasn't the exact opposite of his friend's premise.

"I mean, what better way to get the measure of a man? If you tell him no and he turns around and walks away to find some other body, you instantly know he wasn't the man you were looking for in the first place. And what has it cost you? A few hours of enjoyable flirting and the price of one or two drinks."

"Not every man, no." Xander wasn't sure how to explain the situation to Eric. "Obviously, you're not like that and you drink here. I'm just not sure how to meet these men like you."

"Well, you could try walking up to someone you find attractive and starting a conversation," Eric deadpanned.

Xander shook his head as he tried to figure out what to say next. "It's not that straightforward. Give me a minute to take a piss and I'll try to spell it out for you." He got up and walked to the hallway at the back of the lounge area.

"Hey, long time no see."

Xander had just closed the button on his trousers when a hand landed on his shoulder. He glanced up and stared into a handsome face he recognized.

"Hey, Paul."

"Wow, you still remember my name," the black-haired twink almost simpered. "I can't for the life of me remember yours." He stepped closer and placed his hands on Xander's chest, pushing not altogether gently.

Surprised, Xander took one step back before regaining his balance and coming to a standstill. He'd no intention of allowing Paul to get him inside the empty cubicle he knew was behind him.

"Don't be a spoil sport." Paul pouted. "I just want you to suck me. I may not remember your name, but I do have a clear recollection of that clever mouth of yours on my dick."

Paul pushed again, but Xander was now well prepared for the move and stood his ground before grabbing Paul's hands with his own and pulling them away.

"Leave me alone, okay. It's not going to happen tonight." As he walked past Paul and out of the bathroom the muttered *'bastard'* didn't escape him. Then again, he'd no doubt he was supposed to hear it. It only occurred to him that he hadn't needed his tattoo during his encounter with Paul, when he entered the bar again and spotted Eric in conversation with a large and not unattractive man. Xander smiled. This might well turn out to be his opportunity to find out exactly how Eric went about turning what was clearly an attempt to pick him up into a future date. Paul, on the other hand, had not been in the market for dating, proving the point Xander had been trying to make to Eric.

As Xander went back to the table, he noticed the large man crowding Eric. Xander doubted that others would see it, but he realized instantly that his friend wasn't entirely comfortable. The forced but polite smile on his face, the stiffness in his shoulders and the way he gripped his empty pint glass were all clear indications he was far from relaxed.

"I'm back," Xander announced his return in a loud and cheerful voice.

"Move along." The large man all but growled at Xander. "This is a party for two. Go find your own entertainment."

"Hey" — the smile slipped from Eric's face — "that's my friend you're talking to. We came here together and we'll be leaving together. If anybody is going to walk away, it's you."

Something in Xander's stomach twisted as the large man

diverted his attention from him to Eric.

"What are you? A tease?" The man radiated anger. "You don't get to flirt with me and then ignore me. You all but invited me over. Stop messing with me."

Confusion flashed across Eric's face before his features hardened again. "Fuck off. You're having me on, right? What flirting? We've barely talked for five minutes."

Xander's heart sank. Clearly he wasn't going to learn anything from Eric while his friend was in the middle of discovering the reality of Xander's sex life.

"Nobody plays games with me." The tall man lowered his hand and squeezed Eric's balls. Xander saw the pain-filled grimace on his friend's face before a red haze dulled his vision.

"Get your fucking hands off him." Xander pushed himself between Eric and the man and raised his right arm, only vaguely aware of Eric trying to pull him away. He squinted at the larger man's face and imagined slamming his fist into his nose. His gaze moved to his hand, balled into a fist in front of his chest. As soon as he saw the bandage the red haze lifted and he relaxed his fingers without unfurling his fist.

"Okay, that's enough." A man in a suit walked up to them. "Either stop or take it outside." A bouncer. Xander was barely aware of the large man who'd accosted Eric backing away with his hands up, as he stared at his own hand in wonder. He knew, without a shadow of a doubt, he wouldn't have landed the punch. The bandage had pulled him out of his rage as surely as if it had physically restrained him.

"Let's go home."

"What?" Xander turned to Eric who looked a bit white around the eyes and unhappy.

"I've had enough. Let's go back to the house. We've got beer in the fridge." Eric's sentences were short and clipped, as if he had a problem keeping a handle on his temper.

"Sure." Xander'd had enough, too. Between Paul in the

bathroom and this second encounter, he suddenly wished the bet did allow him to just stop going out for a month.

"Okay. So maybe it's not quite as straightforward as I made it sound," Eric conceded.

* * * *

It had taken them forty minutes to get back to Xander's apartment where they were now sitting on the couch with beers in their hands and the television on but muted. Eric hadn't said a word during the walk home, obviously lost in his thoughts, and Xander had been happy to leave him to it. Anything he might have said would have sounded too much like 'I told you so'.

"It wasn't always like this, was it?"

Xander didn't like the pinched look on Eric's face. "I don't think so. Then again, it's possible it just didn't matter because we were younger?"

"No." Eric stared straight ahead at the flickering television screen but Xander doubted he actually saw anything. "I'm sure it was never this bad. I've said no to men in the past and it has never led to aggression."

"You're probably right," Xander said. "It's been a gradual transition." *And the same is true for me.* The realization shocked Xander. He'd no idea how he'd failed to notice it in the past but all of it was suddenly as clear as crystal to him. He'd just gone along with whatever other people expected from him, and that was where he'd gone wrong. Until Eric had opened his mouth he'd been vaguely aware of feeling unfulfilled but he'd never stopped to ask why that was, or what he could do about it.

"What's going on inside your head?" Eric interrupted Xander's moment of revelation.

"Why do you ask?"

"You have this 'aha' expression on your face. As if you suddenly understand something you've been wondering about for a while." Eric explained.

"Quite the opposite," Xander laughed at Eric's surprised expression. "I hadn't been wondering about this at all. That's the problem."

Eric stared at him as if he'd grown a second head.

"What I mean is, I never stopped to consider the possibility that my hook-ups weren't so much a decision on my part but more a case of me taking the road of least resistance. You know, it's almost always easier to go along with other people's plans than to upset the apple cart. I mean" — Xander smiled at the memory — "isn't that exactly how I ended up getting a lift home from the *gardai*, years ago? Following a certain friend of mine? And some would say I'm doing the same thing now with the bet and the tattoo. You could say I'm once again pursuing somebody else's plan for me."

Eric looked pained. "You realize that was not what I meant to do, right?"

"Of course I do." Xander was horrified when he realized Eric had interpreted his words as an accusation. "And I accepted happily enough. Besides, it's nobody's fault but my own if I am a bit suggestible."

"Anyway, we might as well call the bet off," Eric said. "I clearly misjudged the situation."

"Not happening." Xander burst out laughing when Eric stared at him with his eyes wide open. "I'm sure the truth lies somewhere in the middle. Even if a lot of men are only in it for a quick encounter — and if that works for them, more power to them — I refuse to believe that we're the only two gay men left still hoping for something more fulfilling than a quick fuck. Besides, I wouldn't want to put a good tattoo to waste now, would I?"

He still didn't want to tell Eric about his anger issues, so he couldn't tell him how effective the small bandaged area on his hand had already been in that regard. It had filled Xander with optimism, though. If the tiny mark could stop him from hitting out, it should stop his other impulsive actions, too.

"The bet is still on, and I fully intend to win it."

Chapter Ten

"Here."

Troy barely glanced at the glass of champagne Lorcan pushed into his hand. He stopped walking, slap-bang in the middle of the gallery, and slowly turned on the spot. The walls surrounding him were filled with a wide variety of framed pictures. Abstracts alternated with drawings so realistic they could have been photographs. With so much talent on display, Troy wasn't sure where to start.

"This is amazing. Lorcan, you're the best." Troy grinned at his friend as thoughts about the problems he faced slipped from his mind to be replaced with ideas about how he might integrate some of the ideas he saw displayed around him in his own art. Provided he could find someone to draw it for him, of course. And found the money to pay them. He stopped himself from pursuing that line of thought. Tonight was about enjoying himself, not about going over all the complications in his life once again.

"Sure, I am." Lorcan winked. "Didn't we establish that years ago? Don't just stand here. Let's take a closer look at these pictures before it gets busier and we have to fight our way through the crowd which will, without a doubt, descend on this place tonight."

"Yeah. God, I feel like a kid in a sweet shop. And I can't get my head around the fact that most, if not all, of the artists will be here tonight as well."

"That's what my boss said." Lorcan shrugged. "I usually try to avoid these social functions, as you well know, so it's not as if I've done this before." A frown flashed across his face. "That reminds me. I'm supposed to meet and talk to a chap named Eric Kavanagh while we're here. I should have known there's no such thing as a free lunch — or evening out, for that matter."

"Who's this Eric Kavanagh?"

"He's an interior designer my boss wants to hire. He's taken a notion that our offices should look more upmarket and stylish. Apparently, this Eric is top of the bill in his field. I swear…"

"What?" Troy asked.

"If I'd known they came with conditions, I might not have accepted those tickets. There are reasons why I stay well away from the company's marketing campaigns, and this is one of them. I'm useless at small talk and entertaining people. Just the idea of having to go up to someone I've never met before is enough to make me want to run out of here again."

Troy studied his friend's face as understanding and gratitude flashed through him. "You could have told your boss thanks but no thanks when he told you there were strings attached."

"I guess." Lorcan shrugged.

"Why didn't you?"

"You were so happy when I told you I had these tickets and you've been a miserable sod for months now. I can push my boundaries for once if it means you stop worrying for five minutes."

"I'm sorry. You shouldn't have to do that." Troy suddenly felt terrible. He knew how much Lorcan hated being forced out of his comfort zone. "We can go. Tell your boss something came up and we had to leave. I can come back some other time."

"Nah. We're here now. Might as well make the most of it. Besides, it says here on the catalogue that buyers can take the art work with them immediately if they so wish. There may not be anything left to see after tonight."

"That wouldn't surprise me."

They resumed walking and started a close-up inspection

of the works of art, pointing out the ones they loved or didn't like at all to each other. Troy slowly made his from one picture to the next, without stopping to study them in detail and sipping his champagne as he went, until he arrived at the image of a tree. It was magnificent. Roots were visible at the bottom of the picture, a few of them exposed, others covered in a layer of earth. The trunk was strong, thick, long, and covered in irregularities, indicating the tree had been around for centuries. The branches reached for the sky as if trying to catch the stars sparkling above them. Troy held his breath as he stared at the tips of the branches.

"I don't fucking believe it."

"What?" Lorcan asked.

"That's bloody it. I've been trying to draw an image just like that all afternoon. That tree fits the description my client gave me to a T. All it needs is an eagle about to take flight from the top and it would be perfect."

"An eagle, now that's a fascinating idea."

The voice took him by surprise but Troy recognized it instantly. Instead of turning to face the speaker, Troy studied the right-hand corner of the picture in front of him. *Xman.* How had he missed it? He couldn't understand he hadn't made the connection when Xander told him his name on Friday. Troy had been a fan of the artist known as Xman for at least a year. He wondered whether Shane had known who he'd picked up that night shortly before he left for Florida, before deciding the answer was irrelevant and he didn't want thoughts of Shane spoiling his evening.

Troy turned and faced the tall blond man who'd sat in his workshop only three days earlier. "You've got to be fucking kidding me. You're Xman? I love your art." Troy stopped himself, before he started gushing like an infatuated teenager. He stared at Xander, once again noticing how incredibly handsome the man was. When Lorcan coughed softly, Troy had no idea how long he'd been looking, but he was all too aware that Xander had returned his gaze all the while.

"Oh, this is my friend, Lorcan Barrett. Lorcan, this is Xander Ekman."

"Yeah, I gathered as much." Lorcan laughed and held out his hand to Xander. "Pleased to meet you."

"And you." Xander turned to his left and touched the shoulder of the man standing there. "Eric, this is the artist who did my tattoo. Troy...oh, I've no idea what your surname is."

"It's Moriarty."

"Eric, this is Troy Moriarty and Lorcan Barrett."

"You're Lorcan Barrett?" Troy detected a trace of an accent in Eric's voice.

"Yeah. Why? Do I know you?" Lorcan asked.

"I think we're supposed to meet. I'm Eric Kavanagh."

Troy stared from one man to the other as Eric and Lorcan sized each other up until a small smile appeared on Lorcan's face.

"Well, this is certainly easier than trying to find you in a crowd of art lovers." Lorcan's nerves seemed to have disappeared now that the awkward moment of having to approach a stranger had been taken care of.

"Yes, I was wondering how my partner figured I'd find you here. I'm not sure what she and your Mr. Connolly were thinking when they set this up for us." Eric looked around the gallery which had transformed into a sea of moving bodies. "I have no idea how we're supposed to have a constructive talk here either."

"You want to take it somewhere else?" Lorcan asked. "We could go to the pub next door. It's Monday, I can't imagine the place being busy and I've seen all the art I need to see."

"Works for me." Eric turned to Xander. "You don't mind? There's no need for me to hang around, is there?"

Troy saw the fleeting smirk on Eric's face as he talked to Xander and wondered what that was all about. Were they partners? He guessed they could be, but if they were Troy didn't understand why Xander had been staring at him the way he had just moments ago. There'd been something in that gaze—curiosity, an unspoken question. Then again, it had taken Shane no time to pick Xander up that night almost four months ago. Perhaps slutting around was normal for him. The idea didn't sit right with him. He didn't know this man but the vibes he got from him weren't negative so he'd reserve judgment...for now.

"No, go ahead. You do your boring business and I'll join you for a pint when I'm done here." Xander turned to Troy. "Are you going with your friend or do you want to keep me company?"

The tilt of Xander's head and the question in his eyes captivated Troy for a moment and he almost forgot to answer. "Yes. I'll stay. Give me art over business any day."

"Says the man who's recently opened his own shop." Lorcan's tone was both kind and teasing but Troy still experienced a stab of irritation. He'd been enjoying himself enough to forget all about his shop and the struggles he faced every single day.

"Let's leave them to it and enjoy the beauty on the walls here."

Xander's voice close to his ear took Troy by surprise and lifted his mood instantly. He turned his head and found Xander's face closer to his than he expected. Those beautiful hazel eyes stared straight into his and Troy lost himself in their depth for a few short moments before pulling himself back to the present. *Jaysus*, what was wrong with him? He hadn't been this attracted to a man since Shane—and wasn't that a sick joke if you thought about it—but something about Xander had pushed all his buttons from the moment he'd walked through the door of Pins & Needles. For the first time since the Shane debacle, Troy could imagine getting closer to a man, spending time together, and discovering what those lips felt like against his and...

"So, tell me"—the gruffness of his own voice took Troy by surprise—"if I were to adapt your idea of that tree and added an eagle of my own, would I be infringing on any copyrights?"

"No." Xander shook his head. "As long as it isn't a perfect copy you're free to do what you want. It's not as if I invented trees or anything. What's with this tree eagle combo, anyway?"

Troy explained about the client who'd said he wanted a tattoo representing strength, growth and renewal. They both laughed as Troy recalled it had taken nearly an hour of talking and looking through his sample books before they'd settled on the combination. "Now all I have to do is draw it," Troy concluded on a sigh.

"You don't like drawing? Is it that you prefer to work with existing images?" Xander asked.

"God, no, I love drawing. I'm just not good enough to do intricate designs. I can manage simple ideas, but something like this requires a better artist than I'll ever be. But that's neither here nor there. I can't afford to hire someone talented enough to design for me, so whatever I come up with will have to do or they'll have to take their business elsewhere."

And wouldn't that be a devastating setback. A large tattoo like this one would be, taking multiple sittings to place as well as an original design, would mean much-needed income, if only he could find a way to pull it off.

Xander said nothing for a while as they worked their way through the mass of people more interested in socializing with each other than studying the art around them. When they came full circle and stood in front of his tree again, Xander turned to Troy. "I'll draw it for you if you want me to."

Heads turned as Troy allowed the bitter laugh building inside him to escape. "Haven't you been listening? I just told you I can't afford to hire a talented assistant. There isn't a hope in hell of me being able to pay a recognized and celebrated artist like you for their services."

"Who said anything about paying me?"

Troy saw the hurt on Xander's face and regretted taking his resentment out on him. He opened his mouth to apologize but Xander continued.

"I like that image you described, the tree and the eagle. I can see it clearly in my head. And I like the idea of somebody walking around with my art on their body. Look at it as doing me a favor, if that makes it easier for you." Xander shrugged as if it wasn't a big deal. "Think about it while I talk to the manager here before we join Lorcan and Eric for a beer."

Lost for words, Troy watched Xander as he talked to a middle-aged man in a business suit. Could he accept the offer? The sensible part of his brain screamed at him to jump on it but his conscience whispered that he didn't want to be beholden to anyone. He didn't understand why Xander would make the offer in the first place. Didn't the man realize how much his art was worth? *Stupid question, of course he did.*

When Xander returned, Troy was no closer to an answer. He followed Xander to the exit, vaguely aware of the people they passed staring at the artist. Xander appeared unaware of the attention and the phones being pointed in his direction, no doubt for photographs. Troy wondered if he was supposed to keep his distance, so his presence wouldn't spoil those pictures for the people taking them.

Feeling off kilter, Troy followed Xander out of the gallery and into the pub next door. Xander's design would almost certainly guarantee Troy wouldn't lose his potential client after all. So why couldn't he embrace the offer? Was it his pride, his need to prove that he could make his business work without help from others? Or had it something to do with his undeniable attraction to the man, combined with the knowledge he might well be as untrustworthy as Shane had been?

"What's your poison?" Xander asked. "And what about your friend?"

"A pint of cider for both of us, cheers," Troy answered.

While they waited for the barman to fill the order, Troy's thoughts returned to the dilemma he faced. He wasn't sure what to make of the fact that he was more excited about the prospect of seeing Xander again than having his design problem solved. As much as he missed intimacy, he didn't need the added stress of trying to forge a close relationship right now, and these feelings weren't welcome. And yet— Troy glanced at Xander and smiled as he pulled his wallet from his back pocket with his left hand—just imagining that blond stubble against his skin had his cock stirring in his pants. He pushed the fantasy away. He didn't have time for liaisons right now. Besides, even if Xander was nothing like Shane and had been a victim of the bastard's happy-go-lucky approach to life, just as he had been, he had a hard enough time keeping Shane out if his mind as it was. Xander would be a constant reminder. He needed all his energy to keep his business and his life moving forward.

As Troy picked up two pints and turned to walk to the table where Eric and Lorcan appeared to be deep in conversation, he made up his mind. He'd accept Xander's offer—he'd be a fool not to—and he'd forget about the attraction he felt. The chances of Xander experiencing the same pull had to be slim to none.

Chapter Eleven

"So you two got your business sorted out?" Xander placed two of the four pints he'd just bought on the table and sat next to Eric, opposite Troy who handed a glass to Lorcan. Xander took the opportunity to study the tattoo artist for a moment. He wasn't entirely sure, but if he had to put money on it he'd say Troy was gay. There'd been an undercurrent of something uncomfortably close to attraction between them while they'd studied the artwork in the gallery. He'd noticed that Troy appeared to have as hard a time as he had not staring. And wasn't that the mindfuck to end all mindfucks. He'd barely started his month of celibacy and here he was, attracted to another man, and not just because Troy looked good enough to eat. He swallowed the sigh before it could escape.

He picked up his glass and took a long drink while thoughts continued to swirl through his mind. After the turbulent night out he'd experienced with Eric, Xander had figured he'd sail through the month without even being tempted by another man. Between Paul's assumption that he would just be available and the aggression directed at Eric, Xander had come to the conclusion it wasn't worth the hassle. No sexual encounter was good enough to put up with that sort of shit. How ironic that only three days after he'd had his tattoo set and two days after he'd decided that he really *was* tired of all the games, he would find himself interested in a man rather than just in lust. If this was karma then she really was a bitch.

"I've only been open for just over three months." Troy's answer to a question from Eric Xander had missed pulled him out of his thoughts and back to present company.

"You've only got three months' experience?" Xander glanced at his hand, suddenly worried about the tattoo and how well it might heal.

"God no." Troy laughed. "I've been at it for over ten years. Started as an apprentice straight out of school. But until four months ago I worked for others. Now I'm running my own business."

It could have been his imagination but Xander thought he heard a bitter undertone in Troy's voice.

"And you're doing it on your own? No back-up or partner?" Erik asked. "Brave."

"Not really." The resentment in Troy's voice was unmistakable now. "Trust me, it wasn't by choice. It was going to be a joint venture but Shane, the guy who was supposed to be my business partner, decided he'd rather accept a job in Florida."

Troy's eyes burned into Xander's as he mentioned Shane and the word 'Florida' triggered a vague memory, but Xander couldn't put his finger on why this story sounded familiar.

"How's your hand? Let me have a look." Troy's change of subject was hardly subtle, but since Xander was reluctant to pursue the issue for reasons he couldn't identify, he was happy to stick his arm out so Troy could study the tattoo.

Troy's hold on Xander's hand felt right, and the soft brush of his thumb across the flesh surrounding the tattoo sent a small shiver down Xander's spine. When Troy playfully raised one eyebrow, it was all Xander could do not to violently pull his hand back again. *Flirting is okay*. The words shot through his head as Troy squeezed his hand before releasing it again.

"It looks good. It doesn't hurt?"

"No, it burns a bit but nothing to write home about." Xander glanced at his tattoo, grateful for its presence because he had no doubt that he needed the thing. All he wanted was to take the flirting with Troy further. Just his luck that the first time in over a year he was truly attracted to a man, as opposed to just hot for him, he'd put himself on a month-long embargo. Especially since his doubts about Troy's orientation had just disappeared and he was sure the attraction was mutual.

"I'm not convinced the image is going to serve its purpose." Eric laughed out loud before controlling himself again and giving Xander an almost but not quite apologetic expression.

Xander wanted to growl at Eric. He was used to his friend teasing him and normally well equipped to deal with it. But he really didn't want to share the reasons behind the image with anybody else, especially not Troy. As he watched Troy's gaze switch from Eric to Xander, then to the tattoo, Xander wondered whether Troy might have already figured it out, especially since he'd told Troy he wanted the tattoo to remind himself to take it easy and not rush into things.

"So, would you like me to draw that eagle bearing tree for you?" Xander said, happy he had a legitimate reason to change the subject of the conversation.

"Are you sure you don't mind? After all, art is your livelihood. You shouldn't have to do it for nothing." Troy managed to sound hopeful and reluctant at the same time.

"Of course I'm sure. It's not something I've ever considered doing, and I'm always curious about new techniques and ways to apply my art." Xander mentally ran through the outstanding commissions he had, before continuing. "When do you need it to be ready?"

"The customer is coming back on Saturday so I'd like to have it ready no later than Friday evening."

Xander nodded. "That's doable. I've got another piece I need to finish first but I'll drop by your shop on Friday afternoon. Does that work for you?"

"Yes. That'd be great. If you're sure you don't mind. Remember, I can't afford to pay you for it."

"I told you. I'm not looking for money. I just want to see if I can come up with what you need. I love a challenge." *And a reason to see you again.* Xander almost said those last words out loud as well, but swallowed them just in time. "How big do you need the image to be?"

"Friday it is then," Troy said before giving the specifics for the picture Xander would be drawing.

Conversation became more general after that and time flew as the four men drank their pints and talked about their work, sport, and Canada. Xander had fully relaxed into the conversation when his phone rang.

"I'm sorry. I'll have to go back to the gallery for a moment," he said once he'd finished the call. "Apparently, my drawing has been sold and the buyer wants to meet me before taking it home."

When he came back from playing the charming artist for the excited buyer, Xander stared at the men gathered around the small table for a few moments before joining them again. Eric, Lorcan and Troy seemed to have formed what might well be the foundations of a comfortable friendship and Xander couldn't help being grateful. It would be much easier to hang out with Troy without breaking his promise to himself and losing his bet, if they went out as a group. And he had no doubts about wanting to see Troy again... and again.

"Shit," Troy exclaimed just as Xander had reached their table. "I can't believe it's after midnight. Why haven't they called time yet?"

As if on cue, the bartender came by their table picked up the empty glasses and told them to drink up because the pub was closing.

"I'm sorry," Troy said, "I've got a very early appointment tomorrow morning and I can't be too tired when I work or my hand won't be steady."

Xander opened his mouth to reply but Eric beat him to it. "Don't worry about it. You're right. It's late enough. All of us have day jobs we need to be awake for. Well," Eric smirked, "all of us except Xander, of course. The artist gets to set his own hours."

"Not fair." Xander thumped Eric on his upper arm, just a bit too hard to qualify as playfully. "You know I try to keep office hours. Erratic just doesn't work for me."

"Yeah, yeah. So you keep on saying." Eric slapped Xander on his shoulder as the four of them headed to the door.

Once outside, Lorcan and Troy turned left while Eric and Xander needed to go right.

"I'll see you Friday afternoon." Xander smiled at Troy and was delighted to see his expression mirrored on Troy's face.

"Can't wait to see what you'll come up with." Troy held out his hand before glancing at Xander's right hand and pulling his back again. "You're probably not ready to start shaking hands again yet."

"No, I'm doing as little of that as I can possibly get away with right now," Xander said before Troy and Lorcan turned and walked away.

"Are you coming or what?"

It was only when Eric said the words that Xander realized he'd been staring at the retreating forms of Troy and Lorcan for a while.

"Yes. Right." Heat burned under the skin in his cheeks and Xander was grateful for the dark night.

"You like him," Eric stated.

"Yes, well" — Xander waved his hand before staring at his tattoo for a moment — "that's neither here nor there for the next four weeks."

"Only as far as jumping into bed together is concerned," Eric said. "And I told you I'm happy to drop the bet. It seems to me it has already served its purpose several times over."

"No." Xander heard the vehemence in his own voice and took a deep breath before continuing. "I'm not dropping the bet. I said I'd last a month and I will."

"Why? What's the point if you're really interested in him?"

"I need to prove to myself that I can do it. It' just…"

Xander swallowed. "I'm not sure I remember how to date without the encounter ending up in someone's bedroom."

Relief flooded Xander when Eric only shook his head and walked on without pressing further. He had a pretty good idea why lasting the month had suddenly taken on even more importance than before. If he wanted a different outcome he had to try a new approach. Troy fascinated him in ways few men had in the past and he imagined — hoped — that if something did happen with Troy it could grow beyond sexual attraction. But only if he took the time to get to know the man first, and gave Troy an opportunity to discover who Xander was. Not diving into bed with the all too tempting tattoo artist was no longer about winning a bet. It was about laying a foundation — one that would hopefully be strong enough to build more than one or two sexual adventures on.

Chapter Twelve

For the umpteenth time since he'd opened his shop, Troy checked the clock. It didn't make sense since he had no idea when exactly Xander would drop in. They'd only agreed to Friday afternoon without ever setting a time and obviously Xander hadn't meant lunch hour. Troy had hoped Xander might contact him to make further arrangements, but he hadn't heard a word from him since they'd said goodbye outside the pub on Monday night. He hated to admit it, but he was disappointed. He'd been sure the attraction he felt was mutual but he'd apparently been wrong.

Troy turned the sign on his door from *open* to *closed* and locked the door before walking to the kitchen in the back and opening the fridge. As he stared at the supplies on the shelves and went through a list of possible quick meals, he realized he wasn't hungry at all. How silly was that? He couldn't remember the last time he'd had butterflies in his stomach because someone he was attracted to was about to visit. He'd spent the morning trying to convince himself his nerves were related to the artwork Xander was about to show him, but he'd given up the fight. As curious as he was about Xander's interpretation of his idea, he wasn't worried about it. The man himself, on the other hand, had rarely left his thoughts over the past few days.

With a sigh, he grabbed butter, ham and cheese before closing the fridge door and extracting two slices of whole wheat bread from a loaf. A toasted sandwich would do. Having to eat was one thing, he didn't need to turn it into a full meal.

As he waited for the cheese to melt, his thoughts returned

to what had by now become a familiar topic. He was grateful he'd something else to occupy his mind besides his worries about the shop. It would have been even better if he could picture Xander without immediately being reminded of Shane, but his almost business partner was clearly destined to continue to play a role in his thoughts and life.

He'd re-examined his memories long and hard and even tried to convince himself he might be wrong but the truth was that he had no doubt Xander was the man Shane had picked up the night of his going-away party. Being attracted to Xander as well left Troy unbalanced and questioning himself. He wanted Shane out of his mind, just as he was out of his life, and spending time with Xander would not speed that process up at all. He also didn't like the idea of picking up what Shane had more than likely discarded without a second glance. On the other hand, if he and Xander could move beyond one sexual encounter it would almost be like beating Shane at a game the man didn't even know they were playing. And that idea was just plain wrong. He liked Xander. He wanted to spend more time with Xander, suss him out, and yes, he wanted to get him naked. Not because of or despite Shane but because of the instant connection he'd sensed between himself and the artist.

The tempting smell of melting cheese combined with almost burning toast pulled Troy out of his head and back to the present. He rescued the sandwich before it turned black and sat down to eat it. His thoughts returned to Xander almost immediately and he tried to remember the last time a man had occupied his mind as forcefully. He'd been attracted to Shane and had hoped their partnership in business might lead to a personal relationship as well. But those feelings had been nowhere near as persistent as those he'd experienced ever since he'd first met Xander. Which meant he should probably be grateful Shane had gone away. If two encounters with Xander had him experiencing stronger emotions than knowing Shane for years had produced, his former colleague was clearly not the man for him.

That was a new idea. Until now it hadn't occurred to him that Shane's leaving might have been a blessing rather than a curse. Sure, it'd been a bastardly thing to do but did he really want to be in business with someone who couldn't be trusted, either on a personal or on a professional level? The answer was so obvious Troy could have kicked himself for not having seen it before. More than that, Troy had laughed at Lorcan when his friend had suggested he might be better off without Shane. Clearly he needed to pay more attention to what Lorcan said about both his business decisions *and* his personal life.

Troy's phone made its familiar 'message received' sound just as he swallowed the last bite of his sandwich. He stared at the number without recognizing it while realizing it came with an international dialing code. He stopped breathing for a moment when he opened the text and found himself looking at an image of himself and Xander clearly taken at the exhibition.

Seems we have more in common than just a love for tattoos

"Bastard." The message wasn't signed but Troy had no doubt who the sender was. A second message arrived.

Good choice mate, the man has moves. I should know. :)

Various possible replies flew through Troy's head. 'I'm not your mate' being the nicest option, but he restrained himself. If he wanted to put Shane and his hurtful games behind him, engaging him now was not the way to go. He closed the message, selected both of them and pressed 'delete.' When his phone asked him to confirm the instruction he hesitated. While Troy didn't want to keep Shane's texts, he liked the photo and the way Xander looked at him in it. He opened the first message again and saved the photo to his phone before getting rid of Shane's words. When a third message arrived from the same number he didn't even open it and blocked the number.

He cursed under his breath. Trust Shane to mess with his head, even with an ocean between them. Three months evaporated as the memories of Shane and Xander hooking up sprang to life as if it had happened only days ago. He recalled how he'd leaned against the wall, his arms crossed over his chest as he watched Shane approach the tall blond man Troy had never seen before that night, and make quick work of seducing him.

Troy got up and placed his plate and the dirty knife in the sink. Not that Xander had appeared reluctant. In fact, he'd met every flirtatious move of Shane's with one of his own. Even in his anger Troy had had to admit the mutual seduction between Shane and Xander had been hot and fascinating. Troy's cock stirred in his pants and he adjusted himself while he ruefully acknowledged that his body remembered as well as his mind. Watching the two men that night had left Troy frustrated with a raging hard-on, and if he didn't focus on something else soon he'd be in the same state by the time Xander arrived — whenever that might be.

Restless, Troy cut his lunch hour short. He opened the door again and kept himself busy with paperwork. He almost forgot about Xander's impending arrival when, more than two hours later, a couple came into the store wanting to discuss getting a special tattoo to commemorate the fact they'd been together for five years. It took nearly an hour before the choice had been whittled down to two designs and Troy barely looked up when he heard the front door open and close, only to take a second glance as soon as his brain registered that Xander had just walked in.

"Give me a few minutes okay?" Troy said, grateful his excitement couldn't be detected in his voice.

"Sure, take your time, I'm not in a hurry," Xander answered before walking over to Troy's waiting area and sitting down.

Fifteen slow minutes later the happy couple had made

their decision and booked an appointment to get the tattoos set the following Monday. Realizing it was half past five, Troy locked the door after his customers left.

"Isn't it a bit early to close up shop?" Xander asked while getting up.

"Not really." Troy took his time to study Xander as he moved toward him. "I've no other appointments today and I close at six anyway. There's not much I can do for anyone in only half an hour." He glanced at the carton tube in Xander's hand. "You've got something to show me then?"

If Xander was disappointed that Troy immediately dove into the business part of their meeting he didn't show it.

"Yeah. I hope it's more or less what you had in mind." Xander extracted a piece of paper from the tube and flattened it on the glass surface of the counter, picking up two small gothic statues and using them to keep the sheet in place.

Troy joined Xander and because he didn't move away had to push up close to the blond artist to get a good view of the drawing. Troy noticed with interest that Xander allowed their hips and upper arms to remain in contact. The moment he lowered his gaze to the drawing in front of him he almost forgot about Xander.

"Damn." The word slipped from his lips before he could censor his reaction.

"What? You don't like it? Did I not get it right?" Xander sounded both worried and confused. "I thought you wanted a tree like the one in my picture in the gallery only with an eagle in the upper branches, poised for takeoff. Didn't you?"

"Sorry. What did you say?" Troy had heard the words and had registered the tone of Xander's voice but the meaning had passed him by. He'd lost himself in the beauty and depth of the work of art Xander had created for him in less than a week. The tree on its own had taken Troy's breath away when he first saw it. Now the eagle had been added, the image had taken on a surreal quality. The strength and permanence of the tree combined with the message of freedom the bird conveyed sent shivers down Troy's spine. The image had sprung from a client's mind and had been created by Xander and yet, Troy took courage from it. The message screamed at him loud and clear. Pick yourself up, grow roots, establish yourself and spread your wings, or, in other words, don't let the bastards grind you down.

Troy shook his head and forced his attention away from the drawing and back to Xander, whose words he'd managed to miss for the second time. "I'm sorry. This is amazing. You've taken the image beyond anything I could have come up with or imagined."

Troy could see the relief wash over Xander's features as he spoke the words. His shoulders relaxed and a grin appeared on his handsome face.

"Phew. You had me worried there for a minute." The happy expression on his face widened before Xander got serious again. "But if it's not right or if you'd like me to change anything, just tell me." He winked. "My ego can take it."

"Well, actually..." Troy hesitated but continued when Xander gave him an encouraging nod. "I wonder if that wing could be repositioned slightly so it would reach my customer's shoulder blade when I apply the image to his back."

"Sure. Let me see. How big is your client?"

"More or less my height," Troy said.

"Okay, turn around for a moment."

Troy turned his back to Xander and felt the paper press against him, followed by a few small taps against his shoulder blade.

"Give me a few minutes and I'll change it for you now. Your client's coming tomorrow, right?" Xander had already faced the counter, placed the paper on it, and started working.

"Yeah..." Troy shut his mouth, sure in the knowledge Xander had stopped listening the moment he'd picked up his pencil.

Watching Xander draw mesmerized Troy. He had no doubt he and the rest of the world had ceased to exist. Totally focused on the paper in front of him and the pencil in his hand, he probably had no idea that the tip of his tongue peeked out from between two slightly pursed lips. Troy tried to push the idea of brushing the exposed tongue with his own away again, but the image persisted. The urge to take the few steps and claim that tempting mouth was almost irresistible.

What the hell is wrong with me? Troy squeezed his hands into fists and took a deep breath.

"How about this?" Xander looked at him, one eyebrow arched. Troy stared at the drawing. Xander had done it. Somehow he'd managed to create exactly what Troy had seen in his mind better than Troy would have ever been able to describe it. Troy could visualize the finished art. If he used the right colors there'd be no doubt what the image represented — freedom as a result of being securely rooted. Just as his client had requested.

"You've nailed it." Troy wasn't sure why he whispered the words. "Are you sure I can use this?"

"Of course." Xander laughed. "Wasn't that the whole point of the exercise? I'm just glad you're happy with it." Xander turned his attention back to the paper in front of him and added a few pencil marks. "If your customer isn't happy or wants something significantly different just give me a shout and I'll make the changes." Reaching for the breast pocket on his shirt, Xander extracted a business card and handed it to Troy. "Here's all my information."

Troy wasn't entirely sure if it happened by accident or if it had been his intention all along, but when he took the card from Xander, he stroked Xander's hand. He saw Xander's throat work as he swallowed and realized the artist was as affected by their proximity as Troy was.

The silence between them, as they stared at each other, should have been uncomfortable but Troy knew anything either of them could have said would have been superfluous. When they simultaneously shortened the distance between them, Troy wasn't surprised at all. The kiss, when it happened, was soft and sweet...until it wasn't. Troy had no idea when it changed or who had been the driving force behind the transition, but within seconds the soft meeting of lips had turned into a heated battle between tongues. He raised his arm and grabbed the back of Xander's neck, pulling him closer. God, the man tasted good. A soft groan escaped when he came up for air before losing himself in those lips, that tongue, those strong broad hands on his arse, pulling him close. He wanted more. He wanted skin on skin, dick on dick. Troy ground his crotch against Xander and it didn't take a lot of imagination to visualize both of them naked. Heat rushed through his veins and filled him with a sense of urgency born from need and desire. *I want you. I want what you gave Shane!*

As soon as the words crossed his mind, Troy broke the kiss and took a step back. Confused and regretting his action almost instantly, he glanced at Xander's face. A clearly disappointed expression was almost instantly replaced with one of relief. This was wrong. As much as he wanted Xander — and he couldn't deny the desire or the proof of it as it strained against the zip in his jeans — he didn't want to make this encounter about Shane.

"I..." Xander lowered his gaze and appeared to be studying his hands before looking up again. "That was... wow."

Troy couldn't stop the grin from spreading across his face. It might not have been the most articulate of sentences but Xander had hit the nail squarely on the head — that kiss had been very 'wow,' and definitely worth a repeat.

He stepped closer to Xander and cupped his cheek. "Let's see if we can't recreate the magic." Xander opened his mouth as if he wanted to say something, but Troy didn't wait to hear what it might be. Taking advantage of the situation, he pressed his lips against Xander's again and dove in for another taste.

Jaysus, Mary and Joseph! Wow doesn't begin to describe it. The kiss took his breath away, as if he'd been waiting for this moment and these lips all his life. He devoured Xander's mouth like a starving man finding food for the first time in days. He pushed in closer again, pressing his body against Xander and relished the moment when the man pushed back with equal force. He'd missed this, the intimacy, the heat flowing through his veins, his heart beating as if it was trying to find a way out of his chest, and the hunger for more, steadily building as the kiss deepened further. Not in his wildest dreams had he ever imagined being with Shane could be this hot.

Fuck. Why couldn't the damn man stay out of his mind? The hot kiss lost some of its appeal as the memory of Shane groping Xander slipped into his thoughts. He fought it, just as he fought his urge to pull away and end the encounter, but he couldn't deny the rush of relief he experienced when Xander pulled back and created some distance between them before turning back to where the gorgeous drawing was still on full display.

"You're happy with the image as it is then?" Xander asked, his voice rough and breathless.

"It's perfect," Troy answered while wondering whether it was his imagination or Xander was really as reluctant as he was to push their intimacy forward. "In fact" — he forced a smile onto his face — "it's even better than I hoped it would be. And that only makes me feel worse that I can't afford to pay you for your work."

Xander opened his mouth to reply, no doubt to reassure him once again that no payment was required, but Troy cut him off before he could get the first word out.

"Let me buy you a pint. It's the least I can do." *And I won't be as tempted to kiss you once we're in public.*

"You're on." Xander smiled as if a weight had been lifted off his shoulders.

Curious as he was about Xander's reasons for not wanting

to explore their kissing further, Troy kept his mouth shut. The less he said or thought about it, the better his chances of keeping his distance would be.

Chapter Thirteen

Xander watched in silence as Troy moved around his shop, trying very hard not to stare at his arse in those tight jeans. That had been too close for comfort. God! He'd lost himself in those kisses, in the smell and taste of Troy. Everything about those all too short moments had been fantastic.

If Troy had pushed, Xander would have surrendered. He stared at his hand, at the small black symbol that had done its job so well when he'd almost struck out in anger and had completely failed to protect him against the charms of the man who'd set it. He wanted to fool himself and maintain that he'd pulled away from Troy because he'd remembered his promise to himself, his wish to for once not rush in, and the blasted bet, but he couldn't. The only reason he'd broken this kiss was because something had changed in Troy's demeanor. One moment Troy had appeared as lost in unbridled heat as Xander had been, and the next he'd seemed reluctant to continue.

He walked to the counter and studied his drawing one final time. He liked it. In fact, he liked it better than the piece he'd shown in the exhibition. He opened his mouth to say as much to Troy before swallowing the words. Troy'd been so reluctant to accept his offer and clearly still resented that he wasn't able to pay Xander for the artwork. Mentioning how proud of it he was would probably only serve to make Troy reconsider their arrangement again.

He rolled the piece of paper up and returned it to the tube it had arrived in, wondering if he could tell Troy how much he'd enjoyed creating the design. Would Troy appreciate an offer to do it again should the opportunity arise? He wished he had a better understanding of what made the man tick.

"Okay, that should do it." Troy moved from the alcove at the back of the shop to the door. "Are you all right?"

Troy's voice took Xander by surprise. He'd been so deep in his thoughts he'd lost track of what Troy'd been up to. "Sure. Yeah." Xander pulled himself together. "Where would you like me to leave this?" He held up the cardboard tube.

"Behind the counter will do, right there." Troy pointed.

Xander came around the counter and placed the tube where Troy had indicated, his mind still spinning despite his best efforts to calm down. Knowing *Troy better. That's what it all boils down to.* For a moment, all doubt left Xander. He'd made the right decision. He'd gotten the right message tattooed on his hand. This was what he'd been looking for, the opportunity to discover all of who Troy was first. Now he just had to find a way to keep himself under some sort of control while spending time with Troy and he'd be sorted. He almost snorted out loud—it all sounded so easy...in theory.

They walked to the pub in complete and decidedly uncomfortable silence. Every few steps Xander turned his head to look at Troy and more often than not he'd find Troy studying him in return. Xander wasn't sure what to do. Should he tell Troy about the bet and the consequences it came with? That would automatically mean also confessing to his past behavior and making it clear that he wasn't interested in a bit of mutual fun. He couldn't burden Troy with his wish to work toward a relationship rather than a hot encounter or even a friendship with benefits. The chances of Troy wanting something similar were slim to none. And even if Troy was looking for stability too, it still wouldn't be fair to bother him with his own issues. Confessing all would require the sort of conversation he'd found difficult with Eric, who'd been his friend for almost twenty years. Xander couldn't imagine sharing that sort of personal shit with someone he'd only met recently, attraction notwithstanding.

Troy led the way to a pub about ten minutes away on foot from his shop and turned to Xander as they entered.

"Pint of cider again?"

"Sounds good," he replied while thinking he wouldn't mind a stiff whiskey with it this time around. Nerves swirled through his stomach. He hated the sudden tension between himself and Troy. They'd been getting along just fine until that fabulous, mind-blowing kiss. Would Troy mention it? Should he?

They picked up their pints as soon as they'd been served and walked from the bar to a small round table in a quiet corner of the pub, sitting down on opposite sides and studying each other for a moment before simultaneously picking up their pints and taking a long, deep drink.

Once they'd put their glasses down again, Troy picked up a beer mat and fiddled with it. "I'm sorry." He studied his busy hands as he said the words.

"Why are you apologizing? You've got nothing to be sorry about." Suddenly Xander found it easier to look anywhere except at Troy too.

"I shouldn't have kissed you like that. I'm not sure what came over me." Troy fell silent for a moment before continuing. "That's just not me. I can't remember the last time I acted like that."

Xander couldn't suppress the small smile tugging at his lips and was grateful Troy was still studying his hands and the coaster he was pulling apart. If that kiss wasn't typical for Troy, surely that meant the kiss had been more than just a moment of unguarded lust. Not that he'd any intention of asking that question, but he liked the idea and clung to it.

"Like I said, you've nothing to be sorry for. It's not as if I was an unwilling participant." He forced himself to look up and caught Troy's beautiful brown eyes gazing at him.

"That I noticed." Troy grinned and the tension between

them lessened a few notches.

I really like him. The thought didn't take Xander by surprise. Troy had been on his mind on and off ever since he'd walked into his shop to get his tattoo. It did make knowing what to do for the best harder though. He wanted to keep on seeing Troy, to take his time and discover who he was, and find out if there might be more between them than one or two impulsive kisses. But as much as Xander wanted to take his time, he didn't want Troy to get the impression that he was playing games with him either. Telling him the truth became more impossible the longer he played with the idea. The whole bet seemed stupid now, a good joke between him and Eric but ridiculous when shared with others. And the last thing he wanted to do was either confess to his less than inspired past or his insecurities when it came to relationships. His mind spun, circling around the same questions without obvious answers while he tried to come up with something…anything to say.

"It was a kiss." Xander shrugged with what he hoped was convincing indifference. "A good kiss, but not something to turn into a major issue, surely?" He studied Troy's face, expecting a reaction to his words but not seeing one.

"No" — Troy's chuckle sounded somewhat strained — "no issues. It's just not something I'm in the habit of doing. I mean, I don't usually jump on men I hardly know."

Thank God I kept my big mouth shut. Troy's words convinced Xander that he would not appreciate or understand his partner-hopping past.

"I'll take it as a compliment that you made an exception for me, so." He decided to keep the conversation light and steer it in a different direction as quickly as he could without appearing to be shutting Troy down. "Stop worrying about it. It was a good kiss." *Understatement of the year — mind-blowing is the word I'd use.* "We both enjoyed it, so no harm done."

Troy nodded and reached for his pint glass again without picking it up as another uncomfortable silence descended on them.

"Tell me," Xander said, scrambling for a less awkward topic of conversation, "what do you do when you're not working?"

Troy lifted his glass and took another sip while giving Xander a look that appeared to be a mixture between relief and disappointment.

"Very little to be honest. My life's quite boring at the moment. With the new business, I have neither the time nor the money for a social life. Lorcan and I meet for a game of darts once a week but other than that, my entertainment right now is limited to takeaways, television and computer games at home."

"Been there. Done that," Xander replied, relieved to have stumbled on a topic with relevance for both of them. "I was the same about two years ago, when I decided to give up the day job and jumped into art full time."

"And it worked for you," Troy said, clearly interested in the story.

"It did. I guess I got lucky." Xander smiled at the memory. "I still can't believe how it happened."

Troy raised his eyebrows before saying, "Well, don't keep me guessing, what did happen?"

"It was one of those right place at the right time coincidences," Xander said. "I participated in an art fair showing off some of the drawings I'd done of scenes around town. A visitor at the fair recognized their house in one of the pieces and not only insisted on buying it there and then but also commissioned me to do a whole series of similar drawings for him and then decided to exhibit them." Xander still couldn't get over how fast things had gone from that moment on. "Before I fully realized what had happened, others wanted me to do drawings for them too, and I spent the next six months doing little else besides buildings and landmarks. And then I sold that picture of Glendalough for a fantastic amount of money."

"The one with the purple hues and the swirls of mist with

mythical creatures in them rising from the lake?"

Xander nodded.

"I saw that in a magazine. *That* is a magical image. I remember staring at it for ages, seeing something new every time I blinked."

Xander was used to people waxing lyrical about that particular piece, but hearing the admiration in Troy's voice touched him deeply. He swallowed, hoping his voice wouldn't betray how much he appreciated the praise. "Anyway, the sale got mentioned in the media and, well, I haven't looked back since. I was lucky."

"I'm not sure I'd call it luck," Troy said. "You're good. It was only a matter of time before your talent would be recognized."

"Tell that to Van Gogh," Xander replied. "For every talented artist who does get discovered and manages to make a living from their work there are hundreds of equally brilliant people who never get the recognition. I'm all too aware how fortunate I've been just as I have no doubt it could all end tomorrow." He surprised himself. Xander hadn't realized quite how much he still distrusted his success.

Troy frowned and finished his pint, clearly lost in his thoughts. Xander wanted to ask him what was on his mind, why he was frowning, but held his tongue. He didn't know Troy well enough to ask personal questions like that, so he stayed silent and waited. At least this silence wasn't uncomfortable. He finished his own drink and caught the barman's eye, signaling him for another round.

"Luck," Troy said after a while, "that's a very fragile concept to build your future on."

Xander wasn't sure how, but he was certain Troy was no longer talking about Xander's career.

"I guess we all need at least a little bit of luck in our lives," Xander said. "I'm also convinced luck more often than not comes to those who work hard for it."

Troy laughed, sounding anything except happy. "If it

requires hard work, I should be in for my bit of luck any day now."

"I can only imagine," Xander said. "For me it was different. I took a risk when I quit the day job but there wasn't a lot of investment involved in turning to art full-time. I mean I didn't need to rent or buy a building, I can display my work at art fairs and exhibitions paid for by others, and once I sold a few pieces — even in the early days — the proceeds paid for new materials. It's a completely different kettle of fish for you, I suppose."

"You could say that," Troy said in a tone of voice bordering on angry.

The barman appeared with their order. Xander reached for the wallet in his back pocket with his left hand, but Troy beat him to it and paid for the round. "These are on me, remember," he said, no longer sounding angry.

"Cheers," Xander said before asking another question. "Isn't it an awful lot to take on without assistance?"

"Doing it on my own is madness," Troy replied. "Like I said on Monday, it wasn't supposed to be a one-man operation, but the guy who was supposed to be my partner pulled out at the last minute. By then, the lease for the shop had been signed and I'd bought the furnishings and equipment. I was too far beyond the point of no return to not go ahead."

"If you don't mind me asking, where does that leave you now?"

Troy stared at Xander for a moment, as if contemplating how much information he should share, before smiling.

"Thanks to you, not in as much trouble as I might have been," Troy replied.

"Because of the design I did for you?"

"Yes," Troy said. "That will be the first big tattoo I'll set since I opened the store, and I nearly missed out on the opportunity."

"Because you think you don't draw well enough to take on projects like that?"

"I know I'm not good enough," Troy corrected him. "And it shouldn't have been an issue since the guy who was supposed to be my partner is great at original designs. But when he pulled his disappearing act, he left me stranded in that respect too." He drank some cider before continuing. "I guess I should have listened to Lorcan. He told me from the start he didn't like the idea and didn't trust Shane. But I was convinced he was too suspicious. I even accused him of being a typical overly cautious accountant. Just goes to show what I know."

The name 'Shane' stuck in Xander's mind. *It has to be a coincidence.* Shane was a common enough name. As unlikely as it might seem, it certainly wasn't impossible for both of them to have had a nasty experience with a guy named 'Shane.' He shook the thought off and focused on the last thing Troy had said.

"Sounds to me you're just optimistic," Xander suggested. *Like I am.*

"Foolish more like." Troy scowled. "Too inclined to believe the best of other people. But no more. I'll no longer give people the benefit of the doubt, they'll have to prove themselves first."

Troy's gaze bored into Xander as if the last sentence had been aimed at him personally rather than a general statement. *I'm missing something. There are details I should be aware of but don't* know. He couldn't shake the impression that if only he was able to read between the lines of Troy's story he'd understand everything the man wasn't saying, but no matter how he turned the issue over in his head, he couldn't come up with a question he could ask without overstepping several marks.

"I meant what I said." Xander decided to let it drop for now. He had to get closer to Troy better before he could push further. If he wasn't prepared to share his reason for ending the kiss with Troy, he couldn't expect the man to open up to him either. "If you need any changes in that design, just call me and we'll arrange something. And…"

He hesitated, unsure how Troy would react to what he wanted to say next.

"And what?" Troy asked.

"If you need something else drawn in the future, I'd love to do it for you."

Troy shook his head and opened his mouth, no doubt to object, but Xander rushed on, "It's no big deal. I enjoyed working on that design for you and I get a kick out of the idea that somebody will be walking around with my art engraved on his body."

"If you want to expand your business in that direction," Troy said as soon as Xander stopped talking, "you should talk to one of the bigger parlors in town. I'm sure they'd fall all over themselves to work with you. And they'd be able to pay you for what you produce."

For fuck sake, what will it take to convince the man? Xander pushed down on the impatience bubbling up in him. Clearly Troy had his pride as well as good reasons not to trust others. *And why should he trust me? He doesn't* know *me at all.*

"I could," Xander conceded. "But if it wasn't for you, the idea would never have occurred to me." Xander decided to keep it easy. "Think of it as a little bit of good fortune coming your way, of me paying my lucky break forward. If I'd said no to that man when he made me the offer, I'd probably be back behind a desk, boring myself to tears in a job I hated."

Troy studied him and Xander couldn't shake the suspicion that the tattooist was searching his face for ulterior motives or deceit. The fact that he did have an additional reason for making the offer, made it extra hard to not look away.

Troy nodded, and Xander hoped it meant he hadn't found any reasons not to trust him. "Okay, I'll keep it in mind, but don't hold your breath. One more for the road?"

"Bring it on," Xander said, remembering just in time not to offer to pay for this round. Clearly Troy had his pride and Xander had no intention of trampling all over it.

Chapter Fourteen

Troy smiled as his client closed the parlor door behind him. The man had been even more enthusiastic than Troy might have hoped. He'd known the customer would love Xander's design. It matched what he'd described in minute detail but still, the sheer joy on his face when he'd first set eyes on the image had astounded Troy. He picked up a pencil and hovered it over the drawing while wondering exactly how to make the small adjustments his client had asked him for, without destroying the perfection in front of him.

Five minutes later he put the unused pencil down with a sigh, he couldn't do it. He glanced to his left, where his mobile lay on the shelf below the countertop. He wanted to call Xander, and not just because he was afraid he'd ruin the design if he messed with it.

He picked the pencil up again and twirled it through his fingers as memories from the night before played through his mind. They'd been incredibly deep and intense with each other. Troy didn't understand it. He never opened up to anyone except Lorcan. What had possessed him to reveal so much about himself to a man he'd met about a week ago?

He couldn't get a grip on Xander, either. Since the moment he'd first walked into Troy's shop he'd come across as nice, polite and very fucking sexy. His generosity only confirmed those first impressions. And yet, Troy had seen him with Shane. Xander had given as good as he'd received in that particular game. Troy cursed. Even from thousands of miles away his former colleague managed to interfere with his life. *Only because you let him.*

Refusing to go down the road that particular sentiment steered him toward, Troy picked up his phone and scrolled down to Xander's number.

"Hey there."

Troy thought Xander sounded happy when he answered the phone and the idea filled him with warmth.

"Hey yourself," Troy said. "I hate asking but I wonder if you could do me another favor."

"Sure, what do you need?" Xander didn't just sound willing to oblige, his tone of voice suggested he was delighted about the idea.

"My client is over the moon with the image you created but did ask for two minor adjustments." Troy hesitated for a moment before continuing. "And I can't bring myself to make them. I'm too afraid of ruining your perfect piece of art."

"Yeah, no problem. I can do that for you," Xander answered. "But you realize it's no longer my piece of art, don't you? Once I handed it over, it became yours to do with as you please."

Troy smiled and shook his head before it struck him that Xander couldn't see him. "I appreciate that but I still can't bring myself to use my average at best skills, on your close to perfection work." *Besides, I wouldn't mind seeing you again.* He left the words unspoken. He'd allowed his attraction to a man to rule his decisions once before and was determined not to make the same mistake again. Maybe he was wrong about Xander. He hoped he was. He wanted to believe that what he'd seen the night Xander and Shane hooked up wasn't normal for the man, but until he was sure, he'd no intention of getting attached to him. *It's a bit late for that.* Troy ignored his inner voice, not liking its message or the implications.

"Fair enough. Let me see. I'm actually in Kerry right now and will be for the next few days. I'm arranging an exhibition here and will be meeting with a potential client about a series of portraits he wants to commission. I could drop by when I'm back on Wednesday if you can wait that long," Xander said.

"Sure, there's no real hurry. I don't expect him back until next Saturday." Troy hesitated before continuing, "Why don't you come at the end of the afternoon and I'll cook us some dinner once the shop is closed?"

Silence fell and Troy wondered if Xander had reasons of his own to want to keep his distance. Not for the first time he wondered about the small tattoo on Xander's hand. Surely it would be too much of a coincidence if he'd picked that particular symbol because, like Troy, he wanted to take his time when meeting somebody he could be interested in.

When Xander sighed Troy had no idea whether it was from relief or frustration.

"Thank you. If you cook as well as you set tattoos, having dinner with you will be my pleasure." Xander's attempt at light-heartedness sounded forced at best.

"I'm not sure I'd go that far, but I do quite a decent steak, or so I've been told."

"Okay," Xander said. "That's settled than. Sorry, I've got to go. My client just walked in for our dinner meeting. Talk to you on Wednesday."

Troy smiled at his phone screen after they disconnected.

"Earth to Troy."

The unexpected voice addressing him almost made Troy jump.

"Jaysus, Lorcan, if I were any older or less healthy you would have given me a heart attack."

Lorcan laughed. "The doorbell rang when I came in and I didn't try to be quiet. It's not my fault if you're so lost in your thoughts that your surroundings disappear."

Troy glared at his friend before shaking his head and grinning sheepishly. "You're right. I was miles away."

"You'll have to tell me all about what has you daydreaming like that." Lorcan grinned. "But not now. Are you ready to go?"

"Go? Go where?" Troy stared at his friend. "Shit. Darts! It

completely slipped my mind. Give me a minute to lock up and I'm all yours."

How he'd managed to forget their weekly darts evening he'd never understand. Troy and Lorcan had been playing together and against each other since they were teenagers. They'd both played on the team of what used to be their local pub, up until a few months ago. Lorcan was still a member but Troy had withdrawn from the competition once he'd opened his shop and moved in behind it.

As he rushed through his closing routine the all too familiar regret that he just didn't have the time to put the necessary practice in anymore, stabbed at Troy. He didn't want to let the rest of the team down, even if they'd told him he was more than welcome to stay. He loved the sport though, and always looked forward to a few friendly, if competitive, matches against his best friend. Except this week, he'd been too distracted to remember their fixed date. Just as well they'd agreed Lorcan would pick him up on his way to the pub. Standing up Lorcan, who could always be depended on and never let Troy down, would have been unforgivable. At least, Troy wouldn't have forgiven himself. He was sure Lorcan wouldn't have made a huge issue out of it.

"Before we go," Troy said once he'd finished organizing the shop floor, "take a look at this." He pointed at the design Xander had made for him, still spread out on the counter.

"Holy fuck," Lorcan exclaimed. "Xander made that for you?"

Troy nodded while cursing the stupid grin he couldn't keep off his face. "My client loves it. Said it's even better than he'd hoped it would be. It needs a few changes, but other than that it's exactly what he wants."

"I'm not surprised." Lorcan chuckled. "With a design like that, I could almost be persuaded to get one set myself."

"You?" Troy grinned. "You've been telling me you'd never inflict that sort of damage on your skin ever since I first started in the trade."

"And that's still true," Lorcan said. "But if the message was important enough to me and the image as evocative as this one...well, who knows?"

Troy rolled up the paper and placed it back in its container. "If you ever do change your mind, you know where to come," he replied.

"As if I'd trust anybody else," Lorcan said, suddenly very serious.

Troy smiled. Lorcan was very set in his ways, always had been, and never did anything without fully investigating it first. "I appreciate it," he said. "But I won't be holding my breath. If you'd been at all tempted by tattoos you would have asked me to set one by now." He glanced around the shop, making sure everything was as it should be. "Okay, I'm good to go."

* * * *

"So, are you going to tell me what has you so occupied that you'd forget our darts night or do you want me to guess?" Lorcan stared at Troy, with laughter in his eyes. They'd walked to the pub, secured their dartboard and two pints, and were getting ready for the first throw of the evening.

"Guess? Since when are you a mind reader?" Troy smiled but wasn't sure he liked the idea of Lorcan seeing right through him. He hadn't mentioned Xander that much in his conversations with Lorcan, had he? He tried to remember and came up blank.

"What? Don't you mean who's on your mind? Clearly it's not darts," Lorcan joked after Troy threw a rather disappointing twenty-six as his opening shot.

Fuck. Troy had clearly given away far more than he'd intended to. Unsure how to respond, he said nothing.

"Your interest in the artist goes beyond his talents with a pencil then?"

"Yeah. Well, he's nice," Troy said, knowing full well that

Lorcan wasn't likely to be fooled by his vague response or to drop the subject. As much as he didn't appear to be interested in anything resembling a relationship himself, he'd always been curious about Troy's adventures in that area.

"Well, tell me more. It's been a while since a man managed to distract you to the point where you're forgetting standing appointments. And unlike the last one, I actually think I like this Xander chap." Lorcan's voice had lost its teasing tone and suggested genuine interest.

"It's complicated." Troy hesitated before going on. "I like him. And I'm fairly sure he's into me too."

"But..." Lorcan prompted while stepping up to the oche, throwing his three darts, and scoring one hundred. He didn't push for another answer until they'd finished the first leg, with Lorcan outscoring Troy by almost two hundred points. "If you two like each other, what's the problem?" Lorcan studied him and Troy recognized the moment he realized what Troy's issue was. "Ah. Of course. Shane."

"Yes, indeed. It seems I can't get away from the bastard."

"You're sure it was Xander who Shane left with that night?" Lorcan asked.

"Yes. I wish I wasn't but I have no doubt." How could he? Xander was too striking to forget or mistake for anyone else.

"I still don't understand why you went to that party. He'd let you down in the worst possible way and you helped him celebrate the fact?"

"Don't remind me," Troy said. "Sucker for punishment doesn't begin to describe it." He picked up his pint and drank before continuing. "And now every time I'm around Xander or even think about him, Shane pops into my head, too. And I don't want him there anymore."

"Is Xander aware of this? Has he recognized you?"

"Not as far as I can tell." Troy revisited his memories of that night. "It's unlikely, anyway. I was at the other side of the club when they hooked up."

"And you didn't tell him?" Lorcan asked.

"No, why the hell would I?"

"Take it easy, mate, it was only a question," Lorcan said, leaving Troy feeling like a little shit for his heavy-handed reaction.

"Sorry," Troy muttered. "Let's just throw our darts and finish the game, okay?"

"Sure." Lorcan laughed and threw his remaining darts before whooping out loud when he scored a very rare maximum.

For the next hour, Troy tried to concentrate on the game but Lorcan's question kept playing on his mind. Should he tell Xander? What if he was wrong and Xander wasn't a customary player? If he wasn't capable of giving the man the benefit of the doubt shouldn't he at least give him a chance to defend himself against the accusation? He wasn't surprised when Lorcan won all but one of the legs they played, beating Troy far more convincingly than he usually did.

"I've never seen you so unconcerned about losing before." Lorcan studied Troy for a moment. "Having problems concentrating, are you?"

Recognizing the question as rhetorical, Troy said nothing.

They abandoned the board to a group of people waiting to play and ordered another pint and some pub grub at the bar before settling down at a table.

"I'm aware I'm probably the last person to lecture you about relationships," Lorcan said while they waited for their food, "but if Xander occupies your mind this much, you should probably have a word with him. Or stop seeing him."

I don't want to stop seeing him. The moment the words crossed his mind, Troy recognized them as true. Despite his doubts and reservations, he couldn't deny the growing attraction he couldn't shake.

"Yes, well. Even if I wanted to have that conversation, how do I bring it up?" Troy grimaced. "Do I just say something along the lines of 'hey, remember that man you hooked up with three months ago? That's the bastard who was supposed to be my partner. And by the way, I watched the two of you while you were all over each other.'"

Lorcan laughed. "It would certainly provoke a reaction," he said before turning serious again. "What's your issue, anyway? Is it that he was with Shane? Because you can't blame him for that. It's not as if he could have been aware of your existence, never mind your interest in Shane, or the fact that you'd been let down by him."

Troy was almost grateful Lorcan's questions forced him to study his feelings and thought processes. "No, that's not it, although I don't like that I can't look at him without remembering that night or all the shit Shane put me through before and after. I'm just not prepared to put my faith in yet another man who's likely to let me down. And if he's like Shane, that's exactly what will happen."

"Hold on a moment," Lorcan interrupted him. "Hasn't he already come through for you with that drawing?"

"That's not..." Troy closed his mouth. He'd wanted to say 'that's not what I meant,' but it would have been a lie. Lorcan was right. Xander had already proven himself more trustworthy than Shane had ever been.

His mind went back to the two kisses they'd shared. He'd made the first move, not Xander. And it had been Xander who'd pulled back from both of them, breaking the contact the moment things had started to heat up. Troy'd been too focused on himself and the thoughts about Shane running through his mind to connect the dots at the time but he had no doubt, that if Xander had been anything like Shane they would have ended up fucking that day, and that would have been the end of it.

He picked up his pint, lent back in his chair and stared at Lorcan. "Cheers, mate."

Lorcan grinned at him. "Take your time, figure him out. I've had lunch with his friend Eric a few times and he certainly comes across as nice and trustworthy." Lorcan stared at his pint on the table, keeping his gaze lowered and away from Troy's scrutiny.

Et tu, Lorcan? Troy kept his thoughts to himself. If Lorcan, who only two weeks ago had proclaimed that he had no interest in relationships, was in the process of falling for someone, the last thing Troy wanted to do was to spook him. This time he would follow Lorcan's advice. He'd take it slow and get to know Xander better. He intended to enjoy every moment of that process.

Chapter Fifteen

"Medium-rare good for you?"

"Perfect." Xander glanced at Troy as he opened the fridge and extracted a white plastic bag containing two large steaks.

He'd both been looking forward to and dreading this meeting with Troy. He'd long since stopped denying that all he wanted was to spend time with the attractive tattoo artist. He found himself awaiting this meeting with more enthusiasm and excitement than he could remember anticipating anything with in a long time. He'd been going over the situation he found himself in almost obsessively. On more than one occasion he'd almost opened his mouth to tell Eric he wanted to call the bet off. He'd lasted more than two weeks, surely he'd proven his point by now. But he'd stopped himself. He was sure he'd regret it if he didn't see this thing through, difficult and frustrating as it was. And really, he wasn't a child. Patience might not be his particular virtue but he should be able to muster enough of it to see this through until the end.

Xander studied Troy as he moved around the kitchen and nearly groaned out loud when Troy bent forward to open the oven and check on something baking in there. The tight T-shirt crept up his back while Troy's trousers were low enough to suggest the start of his ass crack. Xander itched to touch that naked skin, push down a finger and stroke into the tempting crack until he would…

Xander mentally shook himself and shoved his hands underneath his thighs in the hope that sitting on them would stop him from reaching out and breaking his self-imposed rules.

"Are you okay?" Troy turned and smirked at Xander as if he knew exactly what effect he was having on him, and relished the idea.

"Fine." Xander grunted the word before taking a deep breath and collecting himself. "I was wondering."

"Okay?" Troy had turned the gas under the frying pan on and placed a knob of butter in it.

For some reason, it was easier to have this conversation without having to look Troy in the face. "Eric and I were saying to each other how it's been forever since we've been on a good night out and we were thinking of hitting a club Saturday week." He paused while considering that as half-truths went this one wasn't all that bad. "Would Lorcan and you want to come with us?"

"A week from Saturday, that's rather far away to be planning a night out, isn't it?" Troy asked. "Why wait that long? We could go this weekend."

Xander silently cursed himself. He should have waited before making the suggestion. Troy stared at him, as if waiting for an answer, while Xander struggled to come up with something.

"Sure," he replied, still not entirely sure how he would finish the sentence. "It's just that I hope to have something to celebrate come the weekend after next." Xander wasn't surprised when Troy raised an eyebrow in response to that statement. "I don't want to jinx it, so I'm not saying anything else," he muttered in the end.

Troy shrugged and turned back to the cooker, dropping the steaks into the pan. Moments later the smell of frying red meat filled the kitchen. "Sure, next Saturday works for me. I'll mention it to Lorcan when I next see him, if you want."

Silence fell as Troy concentrated on his cooking. When he turned the steaks over, he picked up the thread of the conversation again. "It's been a while since I've been out partying and I can't wait to find out what you'll be celebrating. You are going to reveal the big mystery then, aren't you?"

Shit, bollix, fuck. Telling Troy the truth then would be as embarrassing as it would be today. Not for the first time, Xander played with the idea of just coming clean to Troy. Lasting until the end of the month would be a lot easier if Troy was in on the game. But then, would it still be his achievement if Troy accommodated the terms of the bet? Besides, Xander needed to be sure that Troy would stick around even if there wasn't any full-on sex involved. The moment Troy had kissed him, it had stopped being just about not picking someone up. Xander reconsidered. If he were honest, he had to admit the change had started even before that, on the night of the exhibition. He liked this man, and the attraction grew stronger with each subsequent encounter.

"Probably," he murmured the word, unwilling to commit himself.

Troy grinned at him. "Now I'm truly intrigued. You're turning into quite a man of mystery here." As soon as he finished the sentence, the grin faded and Troy returned his focus to the steaks, frying in the pan.

The words to ask Troy what was on his mind burned on Xander's tongue but he swallowed them. If he wasn't prepared to share his secrets with Troy, Xander had no right to expect it from him either.

Troy lifted the steaks from the pan and put them on a plate to rest before replacing them with a mountain of sliced onions and mushrooms. "Do you mind getting a few knives and forks from that drawer?" He indicated a cabinet to his right.

Five minutes later, Xander dove into his perfectly cooked meat. The baked potato accompanying it was equally delicious as was the refreshing salad Troy had prepared.

"Tattooing is not your only talent then?" Xander glanced up at Troy just in time to see the shy smile spread across his face and disappear again.

"I like cooking." Troy shrugged as if it was something he was mildly ashamed of. "I'm glad you're enjoying it."

"I'm more than enjoying it," Xander answered. "I'd pay good money for a meal like this in a restaurant."

Troy smiled but didn't answer and the next ten minutes passed in silence as both men cleared their plates until nothing but some traces of juice were left.

"Let me do the dishes." Xander was up before Troy had a chance to reply.

"You wash, I dry." Troy's voice came from very close by, and when Xander turned away from the running tap, he discovered the man directly behind him.

When Xander passed the first wet plate to Troy their fingers brushed against each other, sending a shiver down Xander's spine. When it happened again with the second plate, Xander realized it wasn't an accident. *Damn*. When he'd arrived earlier there'd been no indication that Troy wanted to repeat the kisses they'd shared before, but now he'd clearly started flirting again.

Confused, Xander stopped washing for a moment to glance at Troy. What was he supposed to do now? He didn't want to push Troy away any more than he wanted to give in to the attraction tempting him to throw caution to the wind. Maybe if he just pretended he didn't notice the contact, or didn't attach any meaning to it, Troy would stop again.

Washing faster so he could get the cleaned items in the draining rack before Troy was ready to reach for them proved futile. No matter how hard he tried, every time he moved a dish, pan or utensil to his right, Troy's hand would be there. The touches had stopped pretending to be accidental too. Long strokes across the top of his hand, a finger circling his tattoo and Xander could have sworn Troy had moved closer to him. Surely their hips hadn't been touching when they started the washing up?

"You okay?" The teasing note in Troy's voice was unmistakable. "You seem a bit jumpy."

"I'm fine." Xander knew he should tell Troy to stop what he was doing but couldn't make himself form the words. He enjoyed the touches as much as they frustrated him, especially with his mind conjuring up images of what those fingers might get up to when they touched other parts of his body. When Xander finished washing the last item, an oven tray, he couldn't help being relieved there'd only been the two of them for dinner. If the process had lasted any longer he would have jumped Troy, bet and promise to himself be damned. His self-control teetered on the brink of collapse and he was sorely tempted to give up the fight and just run with the lust coursing through his body.

Xander watched the sink as the water circled the drain before disappearing, not certain enough of himself to turn around and face Troy. When a hand came to rest on his shoulder, he almost jumped.

"Are you sure there's nothing wrong?" Instead of teasing, Troy's voice now sounded stifled, as if he too fought the heat between them.

Xander turned and found himself face to face with the man who'd occupied his thoughts and dreams with increasing frequency ever since he'd first had the tattoo set. Mere inches separated them. If either of them moved only by a fraction their mouths would connect and…

As if he'd read Xander's mind, Troy pushed closer until the breath escaping his slightly opened mouth brushed across Xander's lips. Tempting, so very tempting. If only he could be sure he'd be able to stop himself from going further, Xander would give in to the lure of those lips. His choice was taken away when Troy pressed their mouths together and kissed Xander with soft insistence.

Rational thought didn't stand a chance against Troy's lips and went out the window when Troy's tongue demanded entrance to Xander's mouth. He lost himself in the taste of Troy, delighted in the tangle of their tongues. His whole body stiffened when Troy grabbed Xander's bottom lip with his teeth and tugged gently. *Fuck, but I want this man.*

Xander pushed closer until Troy's erection pressed against his upper thigh, his cock as hard as Xander's. A cold chill of reality ran through Xander. *Just a few more seconds, then I'll put an end to it.*

No sooner had the idea crossed his mind than Troy drew back.

"No!" A frown had formed on Troy's forehead.

Torn between relief and confusion, Xander studied Troy. "What's wrong?"

"Maybe we shouldn't be doing this." Troy blushed. "I'm not interested in a quick fuck followed by 'see you.' Leading you on like this isn't fair."

"You're not?" Xander's heart lifted. "Neither am I." He glanced at his hand. Now would be a good time to be honest.

"That's part of the reason I got the tattoo." He sought Troy's face for clues as to what his reaction would be. When the corners of Troy's mouth curved upward and Troy nodded Xander almost sagged in relief.

"I suspected as much," Troy said.

"You don't mind?" Xander asked as a glimmer of hope that Troy might be the sort of man who didn't look for instant gratification blossomed in his heart.

Something resembling a combination of a grin and a grimace flashed across Troy's face. "I don't mind at all." He pressed his lips against Xander's again, demanding entrance with his tongue from the start.

Xander surrendered to the kiss while giving himself permission to enjoy the heat flowing through his veins and the throbbing in his crotch. He lost himself in the pure pleasure of the moment until one of Troy's hands cupped the bulge in Xander's pants. Abruptly he pulled back, breaking the kiss and creating enough distance between himself and Troy that their bodies no longer touched. When Troy slowly nodded, Xander's confusion reached its peak.

"I..." Xander had no idea what he wanted to say. Only moments ago, he'd been convinced that Troy and he were on the same page and now Troy appeared to be pushing all Xander's buttons in order to get him naked, anyway.

"What?" Troy asked, gazing intently at Xander.

"You said you weren't interested in a quick fuck."

"I did, didn't I?" He looked away for a moment. When Troy faced Xander again, he could have sworn he saw relief in Troy's eyes. Troy bent forward, decreasing the distance between their faces again before placing his lips against Xander's cheek and kissing his way to his ear. "No fucking. But I wouldn't say no to more than this." He claimed Xander's mouth again without waiting for a reaction.

Troy's lips reconnecting with his sent Xander's mind spinning. He should just leave, except that he really didn't want to. Forgetting about the bet and his hopes for the future wasn't an option he wanted to pursue either. Giving up on the possibility of something meaningful with Troy made as little sense to his flustered mind as jumping the man's bones here and now did. *And I'm just not ready to tell him the full story.*

"I don't trust myself to stop if we do get naked." Xander allowed himself to be that honest at least.

"Good point," Troy said before resuming the kiss and pressing into Xander again.

Xander tried to ignore the desire coursing through his veins. Surely he was strong enough to make sure his mind would stay in control. He had to be able to enjoy these kisses and even their bodies grinding against each other without succumbing to the need building in his body.

When Troy pulled back again, both of them sounded breathless. He pushed his crotch against Xander's and smirked. "So we're not getting naked and we're not fucking, but I do need a solution for this." Troy's voice sounded labored.

Xander laughed, the sound coming very close to being an embarrassing giggle. "I'm so hard I fear my zip is going to burst." Without giving himself the opportunity to second guess what he was about to do, Xander lowered his hand

and opened his fly. The relief when he extracted his aching cock from his briefs was instant. Keeping his gaze fixed on Troy's he stroked himself slowly.

Troy swallowed visibly before copying Xander's actions.

Xander lowered his gaze and watched Troy as he gripped his straining cock and slowly moved his hand from the base to the tip, glistening with pre-cum.

Xander realized he hadn't engaged in a simultaneous hand job with another man since he'd been a teenager and wondered why the hell not. As much fun as it was to bring another man to his climax, there was beauty in watching Troy as he gave himself exactly what he needed. Seeing Troy stroking himself, listening to his haggard breathing and the soft groans escaping his mouth, heightened Xander's own pleasure.

"I'm not going to last." Xander grunted out the words.

"Me, neither," Troy breathed.

Groaning sounds got louder until they filled the kitchen as Xander matched Troy's movements stroke for stroke. His breathing grew more labored as the tension in his balls increased. He was close to the edge. It would take so very little for him to explode now.

Troy threw back his head and let out a low growl as cum spilled over his hand and on to his jeans. It proved to be the only extra stimulus Xander needed. His release rushed through his body, making his legs tremble and forcing him to lock his knees to make sure he didn't collapse to the floor in a heap. Never had a hand job made him come like this, not even when he *had* been a horny teenager.

When his breathing settled and his legs stopped trembling Xander tried to turn to the sink to wash his hand. Troy's left hand on his upper arm stopped him.

"Don't. I want to taste you."

A flush of heat combined with a slight and very unexpected stirring of his cock took Xander by surprise.

"Yes," Xander whispered the word and reached for Troy's right hand at the same moment Troy took his. The lazy laps of Troy's tongue over his hand and him sucking on Xander's fingers were as sensual as any experience Xander had ever had. He raised Troy's hand to his mouth and lost himself in the slightly salty cream and the taste of Troy's skin.

When both hands were clean again—that's to say, free of cum—Xander looked at Troy. He had no doubt the slightly silly expression he saw on Troy's face was mirrored on his own.

"That was one of the hottest experiences I've ever had," Xander said. "Who knew?"

Troy nodded, as if the heat of their actions had taken him by surprise too, before wetting some paper towels he'd torn off a roll, and handing a few to Xander. Once they'd both wiped themselves down and organized their clothing again, Troy took Xander's hand and drew him out of the kitchen and into the living room where they both collapsed onto the couch to spend a good long time in each other's arms, kissing and cuddling.

Examining a body through clothes didn't compare to running his hands over naked flesh, and yet, the images it inspired were too delicious to resent. In his mind's eye he saw Troy's lean, muscled naked body. He couldn't wait to compare his fantasies to the reality of Troy without his clothes on, but in the meantime, he would allow his mind to tease him with mental pictures. He might even try to draw him—just to tie him over until he'd set eyes on the real thing.

In the back of his mind, a soft voice wondered why Troy had been so accommodating. Every single time Xander had hooked up with a man over the past two years, the outcome had been inevitable. He wondered about Troy's reasons for not pushing. Maybe *I've just gotten lucky.* As much as he wanted to embrace the idea, Xander couldn't get rid of the suspicion that the answer, if he ever got it, wouldn't be as simple as that.

As Troy's lips once again assaulted his mouth, Xander shut the internal dialogue down. He'd accept his good fortune and enjoy it. Asking questions to which he might not want to hear the answers would be a fool's errand.

Chapter Sixteen

Troy put the last of his breakfast dishes away and frowned. The long Sunday stretched out ahead of him and he'd no idea what to do with all those hours. He almost smiled when he recalled how he used to live for his days off when he'd still been employed by others. If he'd been asked before he started this venture on his own, he would have said he treasured the days when he didn't have to work. It still amazed him how big a difference having one less free day made. Not being able to afford an assistant meant he worked six days a week. The one day he didn't have schedules for was almost disruptive to the rhythm he'd slipped into. And right now, he was more unsettled than he had been in the recent past.

With a sigh, he grabbed his phone and scrolled through the numbers. His finger hovered over Xander's name before he shut the mobile down again. As much as he enjoyed spending time with Xander, he still hadn't completely made up his mind about him.

He poured himself another cup of coffee while conceding that Xander's behavior on the night they'd had dinner together had been as encouraging as it had been confusing. As delighted as he'd been to hear Xander say he wasn't looking for a meaningless hook-up, he couldn't deny that his reluctance to go with the flow and see where their mutual attraction might lead them had also triggered irritating insecurities. *What if I'm just not his type?*

He leaned against the kitchen counter, sipping his coffee, as he rejected the idea. He only needed to close his eyes to see Xander's face and the heat in his gaze again as he tugged on his own dick, bringing himself to a climax while Troy did the same. The memory stirred Troy's blood and he put his mug down before adjusting himself.

He wanted to trust his instincts which told him that Xander and he were on the same wavelength. Surely he wasn't the only man in Dublin wanting more than sex? Hadn't Xander already shown him he could be trusted? He'd come through with the artwork for the tattoo and he appeared to enjoy the time they'd spent together as much as Troy did. Lost in thought, Troy walked to the living room.

He sat on the couch, picked up the remote to turn on his television and flicked through the channels only to turn the screen off again. There was rarely anything worth watching on any of the channels on a Sunday morning. Scratch that, interesting programs were few and far between at any time of day or night, and he often wondered why he even bothered keeping the television and paying his license fee.

His thoughts drifted back to Xander. The artist was never far from his mind these days. Troy's imagination was trying to drive him crazy with graphic depictions of what exploring Xander's body would be like. And that was the whole problem in a nutshell. As much as he couldn't wait to get Xander out of his clothes and see what he imagined to be a beautiful body in all its naked glory, he had to get rid of all these doubts first. As long as he couldn't be with Xander without Shane working his way into Troy's thoughts, he needed to keep some distance between them.

He leaned back against the cushions and closed his eyes as his brain took him for yet another spin through hopes and doubts he'd been playing with ever since he'd first set eyes on Xander. He was almost certain Xander wasn't anything like Shane, but Troy couldn't afford to get distracted by emotions, not while he was struggling to keep his business and his life on the road. He had to be completely sure about Xander before he let his guard down.

Fuck it. Troy's mind was going around in circles, as it had since the evening Xander had been over for dinner. Troy closed his eyes and relived their mutual hand jobs from memory. The encounter had been so hot, so gratifying and yet, as soon as Xander had gone back to his own place, frustration had set in. He'd wanted more, and from his subsequent phone conversations with Xander. He'd deduced they had both experienced it as such. He remembered Xander's taste and creamy texture on his tongue and couldn't wait for the moment he would be able to properly indulge. It took so little for Troy to imagine what it would be like to stretch his lips around the gorgeous cock he'd only been allowed to admire from a distance—like a kid in a toyshop, look but don't touch.

Almost involuntarily, Troy's moved from his thigh to his crotch. Slow strokes over the thin material of his boxer briefs only made his longing worse. He'd taken himself in hand so often over the past few days—sometimes while on the phone with Xander but mostly when he'd been on his own. His memories got the better of him. Troy stopped trying to resist the urge and pushed his hand down the front of his underpants and softly squeezed his now rock hard cock. Closing his eyes, he lost himself in the sensations while his mind conjured up images of Xander being the one touching him. It didn't take long these days. Within minutes he felt his orgasm rising. So close, so very close...

The harsh sound of his ringtone shook Troy out of his reverie. Without looking at the display, Troy answered the call.

"What?" He growled the word.

"Oops. Is this a case of bad timing?" Lorcan's voice, filled with humor, reached out to Troy.

"Nah, you're fine." Troy scrambled to get his mind and mouth back to the reality of the present moment. "What's up?"

"I wondered if you had plans for today. I heard there are a few new artists displaying their work at the Stephen's Green fair. We could check them out if you're up for it."

"God, yes. That's a brilliant idea." Troy reigned himself in before he continued gushing. Just because Lorcan was his best friend, didn't mean Troy wanted him to realize how badly he needed to be entertained.

"I love your enthusiasm. I can't begin to imagine what has you so eager for a distraction." The joking sound in Lorcan's voice made it very clear he knew exactly why Troy had jumped on the idea and he smiled. He wasn't surprised that Lorcan saw and heard right through him.

Two minutes later, all details had been arranged and Troy went to the bathroom. His day suddenly had a purpose and didn't stretch endlessly ahead of him anymore. He had a hand job to finish and a friend to meet. Things were definitely looking up.

* * * *

When Troy picked up his phone an hour later, ready to walk out the door and meet Lorcan, he noticed he'd missed a text message from a number he didn't recognize. His mood soured as soon as he realized who'd sent it.

Hey, mate. How r u? I'm home from Florida and I'll be in Dublin for a few days. Wanna meet up?

Bloody Shane. So much for blocking the American number. Obviously Shane was either borrowing a phone or had gotten himself an Irish SIM card. How was Troy ever going to banish him from his thoughts if the man wouldn't take no for an answer and stay away? There was no way Troy wanted to see him. He wouldn't allow him to interfere with his life again.

Not really. Troy hit send before adding the number to his blocked list, too. There was so much more he could have said but it wasn't worth it. The best way to stop Shane from affecting his mood was to ignore him. Troy sighed. His habit of always giving people the benefit of the doubt and trusting them until they'd proved themselves untrustworthy had bitten him in the arse hard when it came to Shane. But, while Troy might be slow to catch on, he wasn't stupid and he'd no intention of putting himself in a situation where he would more than likely face conflict. The last thing he needed was to hear Shane's no doubt enthusiastic stories about life as a tattoo artist in Florida, while Troy was fighting very hard to get what was supposed to have been their joint business off the ground. Not to mention that Troy was convinced that seeing Shane again would only reignite the doubts he'd had about Xander, and that wasn't fair to the artist.

When he closed the door behind him and stepped out into a surprisingly sunny Dublin street, Troy's mood had dipped. Squaring his shoulders, he made up his mind to stop giving Shane the power to interfere with his life and moods. He was going to enjoy his day with Lorcan if it killed him.

* * * *

"The mixture of rubbish and sheer talent will never cease to amaze me."

After a lengthy brunch, they'd taken their time walking along the outside of Stephen's Green, studying the art work attached to the railing surrounding the park. The mild temperature combined with hazy sunshine had brought the crowds. A trio of buskers played cover versions of popular songs, giving the pleasant day an almost festive atmosphere.

"Right?" Troy laughed out loud when Lorcan perfectly worded his own sentiments. "But I guess that's what you have to expect with events like this where everybody who imagines themselves an artist can participate." He stared at a display of what appeared to be drawings created by a rather incompetent two-year-old. "Mind you, what looks like a talentless waste of paper to us may well be somebody else's idea of beauty."

As if to prove Troy's point for him, an elderly lady

walked to the display in question and inquired about the price of a drawing Troy found particularly awful. Shaking his head, Troy rushed to follow Lorcan who'd moved on, only to stop in his tracks when he spotted him chatting to two men. One of them was Xander, and Troy cursed his treacherous heart when it skipped a few beats. It wasn't Xander who had Lorcan's rapt attention though—that had been reserved for Xander's friend, Eric, if Troy remembered the name correctly.

Fully aware of Xander's undivided attention, Troy took his time strolling up to where the three men were talking. He couldn't imagine ever getting tired of looking at Xander. If Troy had been asked to describe a Viking in detail, Xander would have been the image in his mind. Tall, with long blond hair and broad shoulders, Xander could have stepped straight out of an episode of the television series, except that he was clean-shaven. Troy's mind went into overdrive as he imagined what a bearded Xander would look like and what his chances were of persuading him to stop shaving for a while.

"Hey, handsome." Xander's voice was soft, as was the brush of his lips against Troy's and both filled Troy with warmth. As much as he'd told himself that not seeing Xander might be easier than spending time together while he tried to sort out his doubts, Troy had to admit his day had become brighter now they'd run into each other.

"Imagine meeting you here." Troy grinned. "But I guess it isn't a surprise at all. You're not displaying your work?"

"No," Xander answered. "It's really not worth my while. I don't want to sound too full of myself, but people who want to buy my work or inquire about a commission have no problem finding me." He shrugged. "Besides, displaying art in the open air in Ireland is a nightmare most of the time. Today may be sunny, but most days you spend more time covering and uncovering your work than you do selling it. What's more, this time of year sunny doesn't equal warm. You could freeze your balls off standing still all day while waiting for potential, but more than likely elusive, buyers."

Distracted by the idea of frozen balls in need of heating up, Troy nodded. He'd just managed to shake the image and was about to answer when Lorcan turned away from Eric and addressed him.

"Eric's invited us to dinner at his place. Are you up for it?"

For the second time, Troy opened his mouth to speak only to be interrupted before he could get the first word out.

"His place?" Xander raised an eyebrow. "Did Eric mention he's staying with me right now?"

Troy looked from Xander to Lorcan and finally at Eric and couldn't suppress a smile. Sheepish wasn't a strong enough word to describe the expression on Lorcan and Eric's faces.

"Jaysus." Eric's voice sounded gruff, as if he wanted to hide his embarrassment. "Don't be a dick. I just thought it might be nice to go back to the apartment and relax for the evening."

Xander laughed out loud. "I love the idea. Let's do that. We'll have to order in because unless you managed to hit the shops yesterday, we don't have enough real food in the house right now to feed four, but if we're all okay with that..."

"You bastard." Eric punched Xander's arm while the grin on his face belied the sentiment behind the action. "Way to make a man feel bad about not having his own place."

* * * *

When he entered Xander's apartment, carrying one of three six packs of beer they'd picked up along the way, Troy couldn't stop himself from frowning. Xander's apartment was a lot like the one he had been forced to sell in order to free up funds. His hadn't been quite as luxurious but the layout was close enough to pull him up short and remind him how much he missed his old place. In fairness, the rooms behind the shop weren't too bad. He really liked the high ceilings and his bedroom was wonderful and bright, when he remembered to open the curtains. He also didn't miss the stairs he used to have to climb in order to get home. But there was no denying he had a lot less space now and he resented the fact that he'd had no choice but to live there.

Aware that he'd stopped moving while Eric and Lorcan walked past him to what he guessed was the living room and that Xander was staring at him, Troy forced his features to relax. His situation was what it was and he couldn't see it change in the foreseeable future so there was little point obsessing about it. Ruining what had every potential of being a wonderful evening with friends made even less sense. Troy followed the others while liberating a can from the pack he was holding and offering it up. "Anyone for a beer?"

Chapter Seventeen

Xander accepted the beer Troy held out to him without a word. He'd observed Troy as a myriad of emotions had swept across his face. He'd seemed fine and in a wonderful mood until the moment they'd stepped into Xander's apartment, when his face had suddenly clouded over.

Xander glanced at his familiar surroundings, wondering what could have caused offense but he had no idea. His apartment wasn't squeaky clean but it wasn't dirty or cluttered by anybody's standards. As far as he could tell his house looked comfortable and lived in—as a home should be. But something about it had bothered the man he was growing closer to every time they met. If they'd been on their own he would have asked what was wrong. Having Lorcan and Eric present as well meant he kept his mouth shut, even if he did suspect those two men were so busy eyeing each other up that they might well be oblivious to anything else going on around them. The idea brought a smile to Xander's face. Wouldn't it be nice if Eric found a connection of his own as a result of their bet and Xander's subsequent tattoo?

"So, what do we want to eat? I have an Italian, Chinese and Thai restaurant on speed dial."

Xander fully expected a long and torturous discussion before any agreement on the food they would order could be reached, and was happily surprised when they all agreed on pizza straight away. He made the call while the others settled themselves.

He smiled again when he walked in and noticed Lorcan and Eric on one of his two three-seater couches. They weren't quite touching but they weren't using the wealth of space on the couch to its full advantage, either. Not that either of the men appeared to be aware of the fact that they'd gravitated toward each other.

"Your boss is a dick," Eric stated.

"Tell me about it. He's a pain in the proverbial, but the job is good so I just put up with him," Lorcan replied.

Oh, yes. Xander would be encouraging that particular development. Eric might not have said anything specific on the topic, but after their disastrous night out over two weeks earlier, Xander wanted his friend to find someone he could connect with as much as he'd wanted it for himself.

"Pizzas are on their way. It will take half an hour or so." Xander laughed out loud when both Lorcan and Eric turned to him with mildly surprised expressions on their faces, as if they'd forgotten there were other people in the room with them. "Don't mind me" — Xander picked up his can and took a long drink from his beer before winking at Eric — "continue your conversation and just pretend we're not here." The grin erupting on Troy's face indicated his thoughts mirrored Xander's.

"Did you say you have your studio here, too?" Troy asked.

"Yes, in the room off my bedroom. I'll show you if you're interested." Just mentioning his bedroom was enough to make his heart rate speed up.

"Yes, I'd love to see where you work your magic." Troy got up again.

"Hmmm, hate to be a spoilsport." Eric clearly struggled to keep his laughter contained.

Heat rose to Xander's cheeks and he scrambled for something to say without giving the game away. He'd tell Troy about the bet, but not until it was behind him.

"Spoilsport?" Troy looked at Eric before turning his gaze to Xander. "Is there something you'd like to share with me?"

"Never mind him," Xander said while throwing a warning

frown in Eric's direction. "He's just trying to be funny."

"There's nothing trying about me." Eric smirked. "Go ahead, show your boyfriend around."

Boyfriend? Xander liked the idea of that and the joy it aroused in him. He glanced at Troy, hoping he wouldn't be offended and let out a slow breath of relief when he saw the somewhat silly grin on his face.

"Come on." He grabbed Troy's hand and dragged him from the living room before Eric could put his foot in his mouth again.

"That's Eric's room." He pointed at a closed bedroom door on their left. "We won't go in there. It may be my house but I guess he's entitled to his privacy. This here is mine." He opened the door to his bedroom, cursing himself when he spotted the unmade bed, before pulling Troy past it and through the arched doorway to his connected studio.

Shit, how could I have forgotten? He stared at the unfinished drawing on his easel and wanted to kick himself.

"Wow." Troy stood motionless. "That looks a lot like…" He turned a questioning gaze to Xander.

"Yeah, it does," Xander murmured as he let go of Troy's hand and rushed to the board to turn the portrait around before Troy would have the opportunity to study it too closely.

"No, leave it." Troy stepped past him and planted himself in front of Xander. "That's how you see me?"

Xander stared at the drawing and tried to view it as Troy might. The work wasn't finished. He'd drawn Troy's face in full detail but most of his body hadn't progressed beyond vague lines, except for his cock which was drawn in full, glorious, and erect detail. "Most of it is how I imagine you."

"You made me look good." Troy turned and grinned at Xander before leaning in and giving him a kiss.

"Only because you do." Xander responded with a kiss of his own before continuing, "I can only work with the material I have."

Troy tilted his head to the side as if he didn't understand, but the twinkle in his eye told Xander he was probably up to mischief.

"When were you planning on finishing it?"

"Oh," Xander shrugged, "I've no idea. It's a work in progress. I'll add details as I discover them." *Hopefully I'll finish it after next weekend.*

Troy laughed out loud. "Are you telling me your imagination isn't up to it?"

Xander couldn't stop himself from laughing along before turning more serious again. "There's nothing wrong with my imagination. I'm just not sure it could do the reality of you justice. Besides, it's much more fun with a live model."

The words hung between them and Xander wondered if he'd revealed too much.

"Hmmmm, are you asking me to sit for you?" Troy had an almost dreamy expression on his face.

"Would you?" Xander asked.

Troy smirked. "I might. I guess it depends."

Xander recognized being teased when it happened to him, but had no idea how to react to it. "And what does it depend on?"

"Well," Troy said, mischief sparkling in his eyes. "I've heard all these rumors about artists and the people who pose for them. Are they true?"

Xander's cheeks heated up again. "I'm sure I have no idea what you're talking about. What sort of antics are we supposed to get up to anyway?" It was clear Troy was messing with him, and for once he was all out of clever come-backs. Just a week from then the bet would be behind him and he'd feel free to indulge in all the fantasies that had been running through his head ever since he'd met Troy. As much as he couldn't wait to see Troy in all his glory and explore him from top to toe, he needed to make it to the end of his month. It had nothing to do with winning the bet anymore, he couldn't care less about that. He knew it was stupid but he'd almost convinced himself that unless he stuck it out, he'd jinx whatever might be with Troy.

Troy tugged on his hand and pulled Xander closer until their bodies were almost touching. "Rumor has it artists have a hard time keeping their hands off those who pose naked for them." He winked. "Is that true? If I were to take my clothes off now, would you jump me?"

The images those words conjured up in Xander's mind almost were his undoing. Troy pressing his lips against his and using his tongue to force Xander's mouth open didn't help him keep a grip on his restraint.

"Well, would you?" Troy sounded as breathless as Xander was when he pulled back again.

"Abso-fucking-lutely!" For a moment, all caution slipped from Xander's mind.

Troy grinned before turning around to look at the unfinished drawing again. "Wanna set a date?"

"Next Sunday works for me," Xander answered, without thinking about it for too long.

"After we'll have spent the night out celebrating whatever your special occasion is?" Troy glanced over his shoulder

"Well...." He stopped talking again because he'd no idea what to say. As silly as it was not to share his bet with Troy, he'd come this far without talking about it and he wanted to make it until the end without Troy's knowledge or support.

"Works for me," Troy said. "Boyfriend." He returned his attention to the unfinished image again.

Happiness flashed through Xander. He didn't know what he'd done to deserve it but his luck appeared to have changed. Troy had to be curious about the distance Xander had been keeping between them, but he seemed happy to wait him out. Compared to the demands for instant gratification Xander was used to, Troy was a very rare breath of fresh air. And he'd clearly no problem with being labeled Xander's boyfriend either. Puzzle pieces Xander hadn't even known he'd been missing slotted into place. How had he ever convinced himself his one-nighters compared to the pure delight of spending time with a man who looked for more than just a willing body?

"Boyfriend, hey? You know Eric was trying to get a rise out of us, don't you?"

Troy winked at Xander. "I have no problem with the label."

Gratitude combined with giddy delight and sent butterflies scurrying through Xander's stomach. He had it bad and enjoyed every moment of it. *Isn't it strange how life turns out to work exactly the opposite way to what is expected?* The few men who had stuck around for more than a few hours in the past had, invariably, gotten bored with him within a matter of days or weeks, despite liberal amounts of sex. Troy on the other hand, hadn't even pushed for more than Xander had been willing to give. One of these days he'd have to tell Eric that he had been right after all, when he'd advised Xander to try dating and waiting for a change.

He put his hand on Troy's shoulder and pushed until they were facing each other again. Focusing all his attention on his boyfriend's — he loved the way that word sounded in his head — beautiful deep brown eyes, Xander closed the short distance between them and brushed his lips across Troy's slightly opened mouth. Troy instantly pressed back, as if seeking more and Xander obliged by flicking his tongue over Troy's lips, teasing the tiny ring in the process. When Troy's lips parted farther Xander's brain shut down while he indulged himself in the malty taste of Troy's mouth and surrendered to the seductive strokes of Troy's tongue. Time disappeared as Xander pressed closer to Troy, who instantly mirrored his movement.

Their kiss deepened further and Xander wrapped his fingers around the back of Troy's neck, holding him securely in place although Troy gave no indication of wanting to move anywhere. Soft groans sounded in Xander's ear and he'd no idea whose mouth they'd come from and couldn't care less. This was where he wanted to be. The only thing better than their present situation would have been the two of them naked, on their own, in a bed with endless supplies of lube and condoms within easy reach. Next week. Only seven more days. The wait had been as frustrating as it had been rewarding and exhilarating. Xander had no doubt he wouldn't resent a single minute of his moratorium once it had ended. All he needed to do now was keep it all together until he got to the finish line.

More, he wanted more. He wanted to never stop tasting Troy he wanted… The loud ringing of the intercom interrupted both Xander's thoughts and the seemingly endless kiss. Reluctantly he pulled back staring in Troy's dazed eyes for a moment before turning to walk to the hall and answer the door.

Xander placed the pizza boxes on the coffee table and went to the kitchen for paper towels before joining Troy on the couch opposite the one where Eric and Lorcan sat.

"I've got the vegetarian, the meat-feast and the seafood version so there should be something here for everybody." Xander reached for a slice of pizza and settled back on the couch.

The next ten minutes were spent in silence as the four men made quick work of three pizzas. When the last piece of crust had been devoured and nothing besides empty boxes remained on the table, Xander slumped in his seat, beer can in hand. He took in his company, one at a time, and studied the satisfied expressions on their faces. Sometimes it really only took the simplest of pleasures to make an evening fabulous. Great company, tasty food and a few beers, what more could a man possibly want—well, apart from a long night, naked with the man he'd been lusting after for a few weeks? But that moment was getting closer by the minute.

"Did you invite Lorcan?" Xander glanced from Eric to Troy as he asked his question. Both men shook their heads in response.

"Invite me for what?" Lorcan asked.

"We're planning a night out next Saturday. I…uhm…I'm hoping to have something to celebrate then. Troy's already said he'll come, as did Eric."

"Sure, I'm always up for a night on the town," Lorcan

answered.

"I wanted to check out that newish club on Leeson Street," Xander said. "I'm not sure why I haven't been there yet. It's been open for a few months and I've heard wonderful things about it. Have you been there?" He turned to Troy.

"No. I haven't been out for more than a darts game or a few beers since I opened the shop."

Xander waited, sure Troy had more to say but no more words were forthcoming.

"I've been there once," Eric butted in. "It is a nice place and they have the best acoustics. You can lose yourself in a wall of sound while dancing but somehow still have an almost normal conversation around the edges of the club. I was impressed."

"You were?" Xander looked at his housemate in surprise. "Without me? When?"

"Oh, shortly after I'd arrived back from Canada. I think you were in Kilkenny for the weekend."

"And you never said. Never suggested a return visit together?" Xander wondered how much more he didn't know about his best friend.

"You seemed happy enough with your usual routine and to me almost every place you took me to was new. To be honest, it never occurred to me you hadn't been there yet." Eric frowned. "Why does it matter anyway? What's the big deal that I've been there and you haven't?"

Xander shook his head. "No big deal. It's just surprising that you are now better acquainted with Dublin's nightlife than I am, and I never left."

Soft laughter dragged Xander's attention away from Eric and made him glance from Troy to Lorcan and back again. "What?"

"You two sounded like a married couple there." Lorcan's soft chuckles erupted into a full belly laugh. "You should have heard yourself, all offended because Eric hadn't shared all his experiences with you."

Lorcan's remark pulled Xander up short and he twisted

on the couch so he could study Troy's face. Had he also thought that Eric and Xander might be too attached to each other? Surely, he realized they were just good friends and nothing more — never had been and never would be.

Troy stared back at Xander from a face devoid of any expression for a few moments before he too burst out laughing.

"Don't look so worried. Lorcan and I are the same. You should have heard him the time I'd discovered a cool new sports bar and neglected to tell him about it for two weeks." Troy glanced at Lorcan and winked at his friend. "You'd have thought I cheated on him the way he reacted."

"Man," Lorcan jumped in as soon as Troy stopped talking. "That might as well have been cheating. How could you possibly have forgotten to tell me about that place and all those dart boards?"

Troy shrugged and smiled. "Slipped my mind."

"You play darts?" Eric asked Lorcan.

"Yes. I love it. Why, do you play, too?"

"No." Eric chuckled. "I've never even held a dart in my hand. I watch it on TV sometimes, though, and it looks fun. Difficult, but definitely enjoyable."

"Man, you've no idea." Lorcan launched into an enthusiastic and, as far as Xander could tell, rather detailed description of the game and all the wonders it contained.

Xander watched the interaction between his best friend and Lorcan for a moment. He could see it, those two men together. Whether Lorcan and Eric could see it themselves was another matter, though. Xander opened his mouth to make a clever remark before deciding against it. The evening was getting on, and he'd rather concentrate on Troy while the man was still here. He turned to his left and saw the same thoughtful, somewhat sad expression on Troy's face he'd noticed when they'd first arrived at his apartment.

"What's wrong?" he asked while pushing down on the worrying thoughts trying to demand his attention.

"Nothing." Troy focused his gaze on Xander and smiled.

"Why do you ask?"

Xander shrugged, wondering whether he was seeing problems where there were none. "You looked very, I don't know, thoughtful. Sad, even."

"Oh, that." Troy's gaze moved away from Xander as he took in the room. "Your apartment is very like the one I had to sell when I opened the parlor. I guess coming here reminded me how much I miss that place."

Xander took in his surroundings, trying to imagine what it would be like to have to give it all up and not liking the idea at all.

"Don't get me wrong," Troy continued. "It could have been a lot worse. It's not as if there's anything wrong with the rooms behind the shop. It's just that they're nowhere near as comfortable as the old place was."

"I'd hate it if I had to move," Xander admitted. "I'll have to look at getting a proper studio soon—the natural light in the room I'm using now just isn't good enough, but I wouldn't want to live anywhere else."

"Yes, well. It's not as if I had a whole lot of choice," Troy said. "I couldn't afford both the mortgage and the lease payments, and now that I've sold the apartment I've got some financial room to play with. But enough of that." He smiled. "I'm managing just fine at the moment, and I've gotten used to new place. Give us a kiss."

Xander didn't need to be told twice and pulled Troy close before tracing his lips with his tongue. The soft sigh escaping Troy went straight to Xander's crotch and he deepened the kiss. Time stopped, their surroundings disappeared as Xander's universe narrowed down to just Troy's mouth and tongue. He wanted more, closer, and fought hard to keep a handle on the urge to straddle Troy. They weren't alone and as much as he yearned for more intimacy, he didn't want an audience. He could imagine what Eric would say all too well.

All too soon, Troy ended the kiss. "I'm expecting a client at seven in the morning so I have to cut the evening short."

"Seven? That's very early to be starting, isn't it?" Xander worked hard to not voice his disappointment. He didn't want the evening to be over yet.

"It is, and I try not to make a habit of it." Troy sighed. "This client wants to get the work started as soon as possible and has to be away for a week. Early tomorrow morning is the only time he can come unless he waits ten days. I'm in no position to turn clients away, so seven in the morning it is."

"Fair enough." Xander still didn't like it but it hadn't been that long since he would have given in to almost any request from a customer, no matter how idiotic, because he needed to establish his name and reputation. Just because he could pick and choose now didn't mean he couldn't appreciate how hard it was to reach that place.

"Are you staying Lorcan, or are you coming with me?" Troy asked.

"I'm with you," Lorcan answered before standing.

"Lorcan and I will clean this mess away." Eric got up, too. "We'll give you two love birds a moment to say goodbye in private, although you two don't appear to be overly concerned about having an audience." Eric's trademark smirk had once again returned to his face but Xander could read the sympathy underneath it.

Even before Lorcan and Eric had left the room, Troy claimed Xander's lips again while climbing on his lap and straddling his thighs. Xander closed his eyes and lost himself in the sensations of Troy's tongue playing with his, their hardening cocks rubbing against each other through way too many layers of clothing. He didn't like wishing his life away, but for once he wouldn't mind fast forwarding time and losing a week in the process. His hand itched to make contact with naked skin. He wanted the taste of Troy's come in his mouth again, and this time straight from the hard organ.

When they reluctantly separated again, Troy looked and sounded as wound up Xander did.

After a final soft peck on Xander's lips Troy got up and

held out his hand to pull Xander with him.

"Will I see you before next Saturday?"

Xander mentally went through his schedule before shaking his head. "Probably not. I've got two out-of-town meetings as well as a few evening bookings."

"Okay," Troy answered. "You'll text me with the details for next week."

"Sure. I'll text you. I'll probably call you too. Just because we don't have time to actually get together doesn't mean we can't keep in touch." Xander grimaced at his choice of words. Touching Troy was the one thing he wanted desperately and still wouldn't allow himself to do.

Troy chuckled as if he could read Xander's mind. "I'm looking forward to it. Me and my hand will be ready for you."

With Eric standing close behind him Xander watched as Troy and Lorcan crossed the landing for the stairs. Unlike the night when he'd made his bet with Eric, Xander hated having to watch his man walk away from him.

Chapter Eighteen

Troy studied the outline he'd tattooed on his customer's back with satisfaction. Even though he'd worked straight from the template he'd created by copying Xander's drawing, he'd still been worried he wouldn't be able to do artwork justice.

"This is perfect." The man standing in front of the mirror glanced from the reflection of his tattoo to Troy and back again. "It's even better than I imagined it could be. How long until you can fill it in?"

"We'll wait at least three weeks," Troy said. "I want the outline completely healed before I do the rest of the work. It would be a shame to damage what is already there. Besides, any remaining scabs will make the process a lot more painful."

"Okay. You're the expert."

The man's disappointment that he'd have to wait for longer than he'd expected was clearly written on his face and Troy could only be thankful he'd accepted the schedule without complaint. It wouldn't have been the first long and exhausting argument with a client, and Troy hated those.

"We'll schedule a date now." Troy moved to the counter in the front of his shop and pulled out his book, giving the man a few moments to put on his sensible and loose-fitting shirt before following him.

"You know how to take care of it, right?" Troy asked.

"Yes. It's basically the same as it was for the smaller ones, isn't it?"

"Exactly the same. And if you have any questions or are worried about anything just give me a call or drop in."

Troy smiled a reassuring smile. "I don't foresee any issues, though. Not if you look after it the right way."

A few minutes later his satisfied customer walked out of Pins & Needles and Troy headed back to the other end of the shop to clear up his workstation. He glanced at Xander's original drawing which he'd framed and hung up in the alcove, and grinned widely. His luck astounded him. Xander had been the best thing to happen in his life in a very long time. He lost himself in memories and anticipation of everything he still had to look forward to. He wasn't sure but couldn't escape the impression that Saturday night would be a turning point in their relationship.

The sound of the doorbell ringing, indicating somebody entering the parlor, shook him out of his pleasant musings. He smoothed the grin off his face and turned around only for shock and horror to pull his features into a new and not at all happy expression.

"You have a nerve." Troy glared at the man who slowly walked toward him.

"You've been ignoring my text messages," he said, "so I figured I'd come and see what the story was."

Troy was lost for words. Anger, frustration and bewilderment at what he could only see as the man's sheer ignorance left him dumbstruck.

"The place looks good. Better than I'd expected, if I'm honest."

"No thanks to you." Anger won the battle of the emotions. "I don't know what you want of why you're here but I'd prefer it if you fucked the fuck off again, Shane."

"Ah, come on. That's no way to treat an old friend."

Troy's mind marveled at the sheer audacity and he laughed out loud, although it sounded anything but happy. "You lost the right to call yourself my friend the moment you left me stranded on my own with this."

Shane glanced away and his cheeks turned red.

Serves you right.

"I never expected things to happen the way they did,"

Shane stated.

"Give me a break." Troy's anger grew. "You allowed me to continue the preparations for this place even after you applied for a job in Florida. You never mentioned there was a possibility you wouldn't be here. You told me to sign agreements I wouldn't be able to walk away from without telling me about the risks." He took a deep breath. "I don't give a fuck about what you expected. I'm left dealing with what did happen. Whether or not you meant for it to go the way it did is irrelevant. The result is the same."

"Lighten up, man." Shane had obviously gotten over whatever shame he might have felt with an ease that surprised and annoyed Troy. "From where I'm standing, it looks as if it's worked out for both of us." Shane pushed past Troy into the alcove and studied the framed image on the wall.

"That's a stunning image. Don't tell me you did it."

Troy considered lying and claiming the art as his own before realizing he didn't want to lower himself to Shane's level. "No, I didn't."

"I wonder..." Shane appeared to be talking to himself more than Troy. "I've got it. It's by that artist you were pictured with, isn't it? What's his name again?"

"Xander Ekman," Troy said before he could stop himself.

"That's right, Xman." Troy smirked. "He's not just a good artist, isn't he? Quite a fun fuck, too, I have to say."

Anger so forceful it scared Troy, bubbled up somewhere deep in his stomach. "I think you should go now." His own voice, low and pushing the words out slowly, scared him.

"What's wrong?" Shane smirked. "Oh, I get it. You're kinda slow when it comes to sex, aren't you? Such a shame. I wouldn't have minded a tumble with you, but, jeez man, you do turn it into hard work."

Something must have shown on his face, because before Troy could come up with scathing reply Shane turned around and walked back to the door, stopping only after he'd opened it.

"For what it's worth, I'm sorry it all happened in such a shitty way." He said the words without turning to face Troy.

Too little, too late. Troy didn't bother sharing the sentiment. "Just get the fuck out of *my* shop," he growled before sighing in relief when Shane did as ordered.

He had no idea how long he stood there, staring at the door while trying to get his head around the sheer nerve of the man he'd foolishly considered a friend not too long ago. He tried to calm himself down again, but his anger and frustration wouldn't be silenced. He needed to talk to someone, to vent.

Troy picked up his phone and scrolled through his contacts until he reached Xander's info before reconsidering. He'd at last reached the point where he could focus on Xander without Shane immediately spoiling the moment. Troy'd taken that as proof that he was ready to move forward and give in to the feelings he'd been developing. Talking to Xander now would only reinforce the memories he no longer wanted to entertain and could easily reignite the doubts about Xander he'd harbored for so long. While Troy had logically come to the conclusion that blaming Xander for Shane's behavior — or even comparing the two men — was unreasonable and unfair, he didn't trust himself not to fall into the same trap again.

He worked his way back through the alphabet and called Lorcan instead.

"Hey, man, what's up?" Lorcan sounded surprised, which made sense since they never called each other during work hours.

"You're not going to believe who just walked into my shop," Troy said.

"The way you sound it can really only be one person, although I didn't think even Shane would be ignorant enough to pull such a stunt. Besides, isn't he supposed to be in Florida?"

Some of the tension in Troy's body relaxed again. He'd

been right to call Lorcan. His friend got him, and since he already knew all the horrid details, Troy didn't need to go over the whole story again. If he'd called Xander, he'd have to explain all of it, including the fact that he'd watched when Shane and Xander had conducted their mating dance. It was bound to come to the surface sooner rather than later, but Troy did not want to have that particular conversation while he was already upset.

"You got it in one. And yeah, I was surprised to see him here, too. Mind you, I didn't ask what he's doing back in town. I couldn't care less and besides, I was kinda in a hurry to get him out of *my* shop again."

"How are you?" Lorcan asked.

"Livid," Troy said. "I can't get my head around him being ignorant enough to just walk in. He sounded as if he expected a warm welcome, too. How oblivious and selfish can a person possibly be?"

"You know how I feel about him."

Troy was grateful Lorcan left it there. His friend could have mentioned that he'd never trusted Shane and had said so from the very first time he'd met him, and he would have been right. The fact that he didn't just went to prove that Lorcan was everything Shane didn't even come close to — trustworthy, loyal, and above all, a real mate.

"Don't let him get to you," Lorcan continued. "You're making it work without him. You're better off on your own. He'll fuck off back to Florida soon enough, and you won't have to deal with him again. Don't allow him to spoil what you're achieving. He's taken quite enough of your piece of mind and you need to let it go."

"I know," Troy replied. *And I was sure I was getting there.*

"Listen, I'm sorry but I've got to go. Eric's arriving in a few minutes and I'm supposed to consult with him about the renovations my boss wants."

For the first time since Shane had come into his parlor, Troy smiled. The excitement in Lorcan's vote was cute. Troy refrained from saying as much.

"Want to have lunch together?" Lorcan continued. "I could come over and bring something."

Troy was about to say that wouldn't be necessary when he realized he could do with the company, if only to stop himself obsessing about the man who should be confined to the past.

"That be great. See you at one?"

"See you then," Lorcan said.

"Oh, and give my best to Eric," Troy said before ending the call. The doorbell jingled and Troy turned to welcome the unexpected potential clients. He'd follow his friend's advice, keep busy, and force all thoughts about Shane out of his mind again.

* * * *

When Lorcan walked into *Pins & Needles* three hours later, Troy was in a much better mood. Shane still lingered in the back of his mind, but the morning had been busy, he'd added new bookings on his schedule, and time to obsess about his early visitor had been few and far between. Shane had been right about one thing, Troy was making something out of his shop, and he was doing it on his own.

"It's good to see you looking nowhere near as glum as you sounded earlier," Lorcan said as he handed Troy a paper bag containing sandwiches and crisps. "I had my whole 'don't let the bastard grind you down' speech prepared. It's good to see that won't be necessary."

Troy grinned at his friend, who always seemed to say exactly what he needed to hear, before leading the way out of the parlor and into his sitting room, speaking over his shoulder.

"You're right, you don't need to run through that spiel... again. All those earlier times you told me as much must have rubbed off on me, after all."

"Are you sure it's just that?" Lorcan asked with a mischievous gleam in his eyes as he sat on the couch.

"I guess the fact that the shop appears to be surviving has a lot to do with it as well," Troy admitted. "I want to make this" — he gestured with his arm in the direction of the door connecting his living quarters to the shop — "a success because it's my livelihood and dream, of course. But there's a bit of me that wants to make it just to rub that bastard's face in everything he walked away from and tried to destroy."

Lorcan nodded and stared at Troy. "And...?"

Troy had a pretty good idea what Lorcan meant but was reluctant to volunteer the rest of his reasons. "What? That's not enough for you?"

Lorcan smiled. "I just wonder how much a certain artist has to do with your new attitude toward Shane."

Troy swallowed as heat bloomed on his cheeks and had to force himself not to avert his gaze from Lorcan's. "Honestly?" he asked.

Lorcan looked taken aback. "Of course."

Troy considered the question for a moment. "I guess he's as much a help and a hindrance."

Lorcan bit into his sandwich, and took his time chewing and swallowing it, studying Troy all the while.

"I mean, I'm attracted to Xander. And I have no doubt it's the same for him. But I can't get the image of him hooking up with Shane out of my mind. Every time I convince myself Xander isn't Shane, that just because Shane betrayed me doesn't mean Xander will do the same, that memory resurfaces and..." He stopped talking, unsure what he'd meant to say in the first place.

"Did you tell him that?" Lorcan asked.

"No. He doesn't know anything about Shane except his name and that he left me stranded with Pins & Needles."

Lorcan didn't react, put his food down and got up. "Since you're clearly not going to get us something to drink, I'll do it. Tea? Coffee? Something else?"

"Shit, I'm sorry." Troy put his own sandwich on the table and was halfway up when Lorcan shook his head.

"Stay where you are. I'll get it."

"Thanks. Water for me please, I'm all coffee-ed out."

His mind spun. Lorcan was right, of course...again. He *had* to be honest with Xander. How could he possibly expect others to be forthright with him if he wasn't prepared to be open himself? When Lorcan returned with two glasses of water he took a deep breath and answered the question his friend had asked him.

"I will tell him. In fact, I'll tell him Saturday. It's not a conversation I want to have over the phone and I won't see him until then, but we have known each other for about a month, and that has to be long enough to share that sort of personal stuff."

Lorcan's expression showed his approval. "Good idea. You can't get upset about others not sharing information with you if you're doing the same thing."

"Talking about that," Troy said. "I was wondering," Troy hesitated before allowing curiosity to push him forward. "Xander told me he may have something to celebrate on Saturday. Did Eric say anything about that?"

Lorcan started to shake his head but immediately stopped again. "He did say something about Xander having more than one reason for wanting to go out on that particular night, but he wouldn't tell me what it is, and I didn't press him about it."

"That's a shame," Troy mused. "I mean, if nothing else, I'd love to discover if it's the sort of celebration requiring us to bring presents."

"I don't think it's his birthday," Lorcan said. "I mean, I'm sure Eric would have mentioned it if that was the case."

Troy said nothing as they both ate the rest of their sandwiches and crisps. He couldn't shake the suspicion that the celebration might well have something to do with Xander's tattoo. *Patience.* He'd wondered about the full story behind that word for several weeks now, a few more days wouldn't kill him...probably.

"And while we're on the topic of Eric," Troy said once

they'd both finished eating, "anything you want to tell me?" he smirked. It was as gratifying as it was new to see Lorcan squirm in his seat.

"He's nice," Lorcan eventually said. "We get on well, and it's been fun having him around the office. He's certainly better company than my boss or colleagues are."

"Why do I think there's more to that sentence?" Troy asked. "It sounds as if there should either be an 'and' or a 'but' at the end of it."

"I hate to disappoint you, but I've got nothing else to say on the matter. There is no 'and' or 'but.'

Because Lorcan's expression indicated that he wouldn't have minded if there was more to the story, Troy said nothing. If his best friend had started to doubt the benefits of being single, Troy would be the last person to discourage that development. And besides, both their lunch breaks were all but over.

"Thank you," Troy said as they both got up and went back into the parlor. "For the lunch and for, once again, being the voice of reason. I will tell Xander about Shane, and I'm going to stop comparing the two of them. If the past month is anything to go by, Xander is not interested in a quickie any more than I am."

"There you have it." Lorcan grinned as he opened the door to leave. "Just remember, it's quite possible Shane used Xander as much as he used you."

As he watched Lorcan walk away, Troy wondered why that idea had never occurred to him.

Chapter Nineteen

Xander walked into his hotel room and collapsed onto the bed with a sigh. He used to love these trips to visit new clients. When he'd first made his name and traveled across Ireland to talk about commissions he'd been excited, both at the prospect of new art to create and at the opportunity to see parts of the country he'd never been to before. It had taken him about six months before he fully realized that he didn't actually get the opportunity to do a lot of sightseeing and that one hotel room was pretty much the same as the next one.

He picked up his phone and checked the time. Two hours to kill before he was scheduled to have dinner with the owner of a local gallery. Two long hours at that. In fact, the whole week had been drawn out and endless. He'd seen Troy only four days ago, but it might as well have been four weeks. He missed Troy more than he'd ever imagined he might and while he had his suspicions, he was reluctant to draw conclusions from the realization. On the upside, in about thirty-six hours, he'd be on the road back to Dublin and that evening they'd be going out. Excitement rushed through his body as he thought about the prospect and the fact that his month of holding himself back would be over then. Not that he necessarily intended to jump Troy as soon as he set eyes on him, but it would be so much better if he could just let go when they were together rather than have to keep a tight grip on his impulses.

He got up, stripped down to his underwear and crawled under the covers of the bed. He'd have a nap before he had to get ready for the evening out.

As soon as he closed his eyes, Troy's image sprang to life in his mind and his imagination wasted no time before showing him pictures of what the man might look like naked. Blood rushed to his crotch, and Xander reached down to cup his growing erection. So much for trying to sleep.

Suddenly thirty-six hours seemed like a lifetime. He picked up his phone again and scrolled down to Troy's number, hesitating before pressing the 'call' icon. Troy and he had been in frequent contact since last weekend. Would he seem too needy if he called again? Or would it show a lack of interest if today was the first day he didn't get in touch?

Xander stared at his screen, thumb hovering over the all too tempting icon while fervently wishing he had a frame of reference for how much contact was too much—or too little for that matter. He tried to work out whether he or Troy had initiated most of the contact between them and came up blank. Too many calls had been made, and even more text messages had been exchanged. He'd no idea if it was his turn again, or if there even was such a thing as turns when it came to staying in touch.

Without giving himself another opportunity to obsess about it he pressed 'call'. Worst-case scenario it would be a short conversation. Hearing Troy's voice would be worth it.

"Hey." Unlike on previous occasions Troy sounded subdued rather than delighted to hear from Xander.

"How're you doing?" Xander asked. "This is not a bad time, is it?" It was after six, but if Xander had learned anything over the past month it was that owning and running a tattoo parlor didn't always mean sticking to regular shopping hours.

"No, your timing is fine," Troy answered, sounding a bit more like his usual happy self. "I was about to take a shower, but that can wait."

"Uhuh," Xander mumbled while wondering how far into

his getting ready for the shower routine Troy had gotten before he answered the phone. "Are you sure this isn't inconvenient? You sound a bit…distracted." Xander almost said 'down' before thinking better of it.

"Yeah, it's fine." It was Troy's turn to hesitate for a moment. "In fact, your timing is great. I had a bit of a rough start to the day and I could do with some cheering up."

"Oh, anything you want to talk about?"

"No. Not right now, anyway. I had a chat with Lorcan and he pulled me back from the edge." Troy chuckled although to Xander's ears it sounded strained. He also couldn't stop the flash of jealousy he experienced because Troy had turned to Lorcan for support rather than to him.

"So, what are you up to?" Troy asked before Xander could get too maudlin about Troy leaning on Lorcan. "Meetings going according to plan?"

"Yes, it's all fine. The exhibition has been planned and I'm meeting my client for one last sitting tomorrow before coming home Saturday morning. I was going to take a nap but found I couldn't sleep."

"You're in bed?" Troy's voice suddenly sounded huskier than it had done only moments earlier.

"I am," Xander confirmed.

"Well, now." Troy's words slowed right down, giving his voice a teasing edge. "Does that mean you're as naked as I am?"

Fuck me. Just like that Xander's dick made its presence known. *Exactly how I was picturing you before I called.*

"I guess that depends on exactly how naked you are." *After all,* Xander mused, *two can play this game.*

Troy laughed. "Starkers here."

"That beats me in my boxers." Xander worked hard to keep his tone light while his blood pressure shot up.

"You sleep with clothes on? I'm so disappointed." Laughter sounded in Troy's voice.

"That depends on the circumstances." Xander slipped into full-on flirt mode.

"So." Troy's voice was suddenly softer and Xander had to strain to hear him. "If I were with you right now?"

Xander's mind momentarily scrambled. If Troy had been with him, he wouldn't have gotten undressed in the first place, of course. He still had two days to go before he'd served his month. Since he'd no intention of telling Troy about his bet and the reasons for it over the phone, and because the whole thing would be done and over with by the time they would see each other again, Xander decided to stay in the game. "If you were here, I guess my underpants would be having an even harder time trying to keep me constrained."

"Give me a moment," Troy said.

"Sure, what are you up to?"

"If you're warm and comfy in your bed, I don't see why I should have to freeze my tits off. I'm getting under the covers too."

Xander laughed as he listened to the rustling of a duvet being pulled back and the satisfied sigh that followed. "Settled are you?"

"Oh, yeah." Troy sounded lazy and relaxed. "Now what were you saying about your underwear? Seems to me you're somewhat overdressed for this conversation."

"I didn't realize there was a dress code for when I call you." Xander reached for his boxers and pushed them down, wriggling in the bed to get them all the way off him.

"There wasn't." Troy chuckled. "But now is as good a time as any to establish one. From now on, no more calling me unless you're naked."

Troy's voice and words worked wonders for Xander's libido. He stroked a finger along his now fully erect cock, teasing himself, and luxuriated in the shivers it sent down his spine. "Don't worry about it. I've remedied the situation. I'm now as naked as you are."

"Are you also as hard as I am?"

"I guess that depends on what state you happen to be in, doesn't it?" Xander suggested.

"Let's just say that if there were any homeless fairies looking for a roof over their head right now, they could make themselves comfortable in the duvet tent I've created here."

Xander laughed. "That makes two of us." He enjoyed the playful yet hot banter they'd fallen into. While they'd called each other often, this was the first time they'd indulged in phone sex, and for a moment he was upset with himself for not initiating a call like this one earlier. Then he let it go, worrying about things he couldn't change would only serve to spoil the rest of this call.

"What are you doing?" Troy asked, his voice huskier than it had been before.

"Teasing myself." Xander stroked a finger along the length of his throbbing dick, concentrating on the sensitive head for a few moments before tracing his length to the base again. "What about you?"

"Trying to stop myself from fucking my hand, now you said that," Troy answered. "I wouldn't mind being the one teasing you." His voice got rougher. "With my fingers, and then with my tongue." He fell silent.

"Go on," Xander all but begged while wrapping his fingers around his cock and slowly moving up and down.

"You like what you're hearing? Are you stroking yourself? Imagining it's me?"

Damn. Troy's words hit all the right buttons in Xander and he stilled again, not wanting the pleasurable torture to be over so soon. "I am. And I so wish it was your hand… your mouth." Even without stimulating himself, Xander's excitement grew.

"Yeah."

They both fell silent and for a while all Xander heard was Troy's breathing, getting ever louder in his ear. He had no doubt Troy was listening to Xander doing the same thing.

"I can't wait to see you, to touch you." Xander blurted the words out, thankful there was half a country between them because if he'd been anywhere near Troy right now he would have told him to come over so they could truly enjoy this together.

"Tell me what you'd do," Troy breathed.

"I want to trace every swirl and line of your tattoo with my finger." Xander didn't need to think about his answer. It had been his favorite fantasy for weeks. "And then..." He lost his line of reasoning as he tightened his grip around his cock and pulled harder.

"Then what?" Troy's voice was barely more than a whisper.

"Then I'd investigate your body. Every inch of your skin until I'd found all your hotspots. I want to discover where to touch you so you'll squirm. And I'd tease you." Xander lost himself in the images his words created in his head. "I'd stroke the inside of your thighs, moving my hand ever higher until you'd beg me to touch your rock-hard and straining dick."

"Oh, God, yeah. Don't stop." The need in Troy's voice sent Xander soaring.

"Then, only after your begging had convinced me of your need, I'd concentrate on that beautiful cock of yours. Stroke my finger along it. Fondle your balls and tease your hole."

"Which one?" Troy asked.

For a moment, Xander's mind scrambled. *Which what?* Then he knew. "Do you have a preference?" he teased.

"Yes. No. Fuck, both!"

"I want to lick you. Taste you. All of you." Xander brought his hand to his mouth and licked it. When Troy moaned into his ear he smiled. He'd been loud enough for Troy to hear exactly what he did, just as he'd hoped. He wrapped his now slick fingers around his cock again and stroked himself more forcefully.

"I'm close." Troy sounded as if he had to fight to get the words out.

"And then I'd really go down on you. Take you deep. Swallow around that dick of yours again and again..." Xander had to stop talking for a moment to catch his breath.

"Don't. Stop. Now," Troy all but begged.

"I'd suck you until you spill deep down my throat, and I wouldn't waste a single drop."

"Fuck. Yeah!"

Xander didn't need to see him in order to be sure Troy was coming. The sounds reaching him through his phone were needy and exhilarating while his memory conjured up images of what Troy had looked like the one time Xander had seen him come. It was enough. With one last pull and a twist of his wrist, Xander sent himself over the edge, as well.

"You still there?"

Xander had no idea how much time had passed when Troy asked his question.

"Just about." He laughed.

"Yeah, me, too." All signs of stress had disappeared from Troy's voice. "Why didn't we do this before? It's not as if we haven't been spending hours talking to each other on the phone."

"I'm pretty sure we won't be so neglectful in the future." Xander laughed. "Listen, I've got to let you go. For some reason I suddenly need a shower before I go out for dinner."

"Fair enough," Troy said. "And, Xander... Thank you."

"For what?"

"This distraction was exactly what I needed. Lorcan may have talked me off the ledge, but this is the first time today I'm totally relaxed."

"Trust me." Xander smiled although he knew Troy couldn't see him. "It truly was entirely my pleasure."

"Oh, before you go. Your celebration's still on for Saturday?"

"Absolutely." Xander couldn't wait.

"Are you ready to tell me what we'll be celebrating?" Troy asked.

"Not yet."

"Bloody tease," Troy murmured, but there was no malice in his voice. "Okay, go and have your shower. I'll see you

Saturday."

"See you then." Xander ended the call and pushed himself up and out of his bed. As the hot water fell from the showerhead to his body he couldn't deny that Saturday night still couldn't arrive soon enough. But this one phone call would carry him over until he'd be able to turn his words into deeds.

Chapter Twenty

A few steps into the club, Troy stopped to take in his surroundings. He and Lorcan had arrived about fifteen minutes before the agreed time, and he wasn't surprised when he didn't spot Xander or Eric anywhere. The fact that the club was relatively empty didn't shock him, either. Ten o'clock on a Saturday night was early. This place probably wouldn't fill up until after most pubs closed at twelve.

The club was huge and cleverly laid out. The dance floor in the middle was large and bathed in bright flashing lights. Off to the left a long bar stretched along the wall. Over on the right he spotted seating areas with what looked like comfortable chairs and couches, while high tables without seats, like the one close to the entrance he was leaning on, were also visible on the far side of the still almost empty dancing area.

"What are you having?" He shouted the question at Lorcan.

"I'll start with a pint of the black stuff," Lorcan answered. "If you get the drinks, I'll secure us a seat over there." He nodded in the direction of the seating area.

"Sure." Troy walked to the bar. While he waited for the bartender to catch his eye, his thoughts went back over the past week. Who'd have known six days could stretch out as long as these had? If it hadn't been for their texts and phone calls he would have driven himself to distraction fantasizing about Xander. He'd stopped denying it to himself after Xander's call on Thursday. He'd fallen, hard, and he was fairly certain he wasn't the only one. He was tired of holding himself back. He wanted to move forward, spend the night with Xander and figure out whether or not they might have a future together. No more *careful*. He'd stop his game of wait-and-see and take the jump. Trusting Xander didn't scare him anymore.

Troy placed his order and watched the barman as he pulled two pints until they were nearly full and set them aside to rest.

"Well, what do you know? And there was me thinking I'd seen the last of you two days ago."

Troy's hackles came up as soon as he recognized the voice. What were the bloody chances of *him* picking this club while he was visiting Dublin? Shane was the last person Troy wanted to interact with. Surely he'd made it perfectly clear he was done with Shane and his games during their conversation last Thursday. He wouldn't have complained if he'd never met the man again, but to run into him now was just too cynical. Tonight was supposed to be about him reclaiming everything Shane had robbed him of. Unless he got his act together, Shane could easily spoil this evening for him, and Troy had no intention of allowing that to happen.

"Shane. There really is no getting rid of you, is there?" Troy didn't even try to hide his dislike. He stared at the man he'd imagined he fancied not too long ago. Shane's ever changing hair was colored bright red tonight and standing up in heavily gelled spikes. The eyeliner and mascara were nothing new. Tonight the makeup didn't enhance hazel-colored eyes though. The rather vivid, almost fluorescent, green lenses gave Shane a somewhat sinister appearance.

"Don't be like that. We used to be friends, remember?"

"You can stop trying to pull that one. You lost any claim to my friendship when you left me high and dry."

"Anyway." Shane waved his arm as if to dismiss Troy's words and almost lost his balance. "Tonight's my last night in town. Flying back tomorrow and I can't wait to get away from this dump. Dublin is such a provincial backwater compared to Orlando. Going to Florida is the best thing I've ever done."

Troy wondered how much Shane had already drunk and whether it was the alcohol speaking or Shane was really going out of his way to be as obnoxious as possible.

"Good for you." Troy turned his head and stared at the bartender, silently willing him to finish pulling those pints. He had to get away from Shane before the man managed to irritate him enough to ruin the evening.

"If you're ever in Florida…"

Troy snapped around and scowled at Shane, his glare apparently ferocious enough to shut him up mid-sentence.

"That'll be twelve Euro."

Never had Troy been as grateful to have a conversation interrupted. Despite his best intentions not to allow Shane to get to him, he'd been about to hit him in the face after that last, unfinished remark. And wouldn't that have wrecked the evening before it had properly started.

Without a word, Troy turned away from Shane, paid the barman and picked up the pints. Walking around the dance floor he searched the seating area for Lorcan while resisting the urge to look over his shoulder and check on Shane. When he spotted Lorcan, he saw his friend had been joined by Eric and Xander, drinks already in front of them on the table. The bright smile erupting on Xander's face as soon as he set eyes on Troy, went a long way toward lifting his spirits again.

"Hey, you got here ahead of us."

Soft lips, accompanied by the subtle scratch of a five o'clock shadow, connected with Troy's cheek as soon as Troy sat next to Xander. The shiver running down his spine spread out until it ran through Troy's limbs too, and Xander's soft laughter in his ear told him his reaction hadn't gone unnoticed. This was exactly what he needed after his encounter with Shane. It was time to take back control over his life, to stop allowing Shane to rule his feelings and decisions. Tonight would be the start of a new chapter.

Troy turned his head and pressed his lips against Xander's,

hoping to share the decision he'd just made without words. Stopping only just short of claiming Xander's mouth was harder than it should have been, but Troy honestly wasn't sure if he would be able to hold back once he dove in. And while he had no issues with public displays of affection, public displays of animalistic lust were another thing completely.

"Hmmm, tastes like more," Xander almost purred the words into Troy's ear. "And I'm so ready for more."

Happiness filled Troy to hear Xander say the words he'd been thinking. He'd known the artist for almost a month now and over that time the instant attraction he'd experienced during their first meeting had steadily grown from fondness and lust into something he wasn't quite prepared to name yet but really enjoyed.

"You want more kisses?" Troy murmured the words against Xander's lips before licking over them. When his words made Xander smile and thus open his mouth, Troy took full advantage of the situation and lapped into Xander until their tongues danced to a rhythm that had nothing to do with the music blasting from the speakers.

For reasons he couldn't put his finger on, Troy suspected Xander had turned a corner, too. He no longer tasted hesitance or restraint in Xander's kisses, as if he allowed himself to get fully engaged for the first time since they'd met.

"Makes you wonder if they even remember we're here, doesn't it?" Eric's raised, humor-laden voice cut through the noise surrounding them.

Troy imagined the expression on Xander's face—a delightful combination of embarrassment and arousal—probably mirrored the one on his own face.

"Young love." Lorcan smirked before theatrically sighing and placing a hand over his heart. "Almost makes me swoon."

Eric burst out laughing and for the next few minutes Lorcan and he had a whale of a time teasing Xander and

Troy about their inability to keep their hands and mouths off each other.

"Everybody's a comedian these days," Xander grumbled before adding, "Wanna dance?"

Troy glanced at the dance floor which had been steadily filling up with moving bodies and nodded. He could think of worse ways to spend his evening than being pressed up close to Xander. Better ways too, of course, but there'd be time for that later. He wanted the full works, kissing, dancing, teasing—by the time they made it to his or Xander's house Troy wanted both of them to be desperate for each other. Not that he was far removed from that point now, but the build-up had always been at least half the fun for him.

They stopped at the edge of the dance floor to take in the people already there. Troy realized he and Xander had spotted the young couple at the same time when Xander's hands on Troy's hips tightened and Xander whispered in his ear.

"See them? Don't they look hot?"

Troy studied the couple more closely. The young man with black hair appeared to be comfortable in his skin, moving freely while making sure never to lose physical contact with the red-haired, somewhat younger, man close to him. The redhead seemed far less self-assured. Glancing around nervously, he appeared tense and slow to relax. Troy was about to share his thoughts with Xander when a third young man, a bleached blond twink, pushed himself against the younger man's backside, falling into the couple's rhythm. Despite being constantly aware of Xander close behind him and his cock pressing into his lower back, Troy couldn't keep his eyes off the trio in front of him. The youngest man had almost come to a standstill when the twink first moved in, but had clearly let go of his reservations now because as far as Troy could tell, he'd lost himself in the sensations. Not that Troy could blame him, those three looked hot as hell.

"I'd love to know what their story is." Xander's words were spoken straight into Troy's ear, his warm breath caressing Troy's cheek. "But I want to dance with you more."

Xander pushed Troy forward into the mass of moving bodies, before turning him around and pulling him close. "Let's create some heat of our own."

The last of the tension Troy had been unable to shed since his encounter with Shane, evaporated when Xander pulled him close and pushed his hands into the back pockets of Troy's tight black jeans. The softly squeezing fingers awakened nerve endings and Troy's body reacted enthusiastically. His cock filled and pressed ever harder against the zip of his fly, his heartbeat grew faster and a smoldering heat seemed to burn its way from Troy's center to where he connected with Xander.

"God, but you feel good against me. Can't wait for us to shed a few layers of material." Once again, Xander's breath ghosted sensually across Troy's skin as he spoke, leaving a trail of goose bumps in its wake.

Slipping a hand between Xander's tight shirt and the warm skin of his back, Troy luxuriated in the sensation of naked flesh under his fingers. He stroked and traced Xander's backbone up as high as he could reach, given their positions and Xander's clothes. Xander shuddered in Troy's arms and pressed closer, making it all too clear that he too was hot and more than ready to take matters further.

"Do we have to stay here?" Troy asked, trying to keep the needy tone from his voice.

"Just a while longer." Xander sounded as excited as Troy was. "We—well, I—dragged Lorcan and Eric out with us. It's only fair we keep them company."

Troy squinted through the bright lights in the direction of the seating area where they'd left Eric and Lorcan talking to each other. Sure enough, there they were. Heads close together, they appeared to be engrossed in whatever they were talking about…or each other. Wouldn't that be a turn-up for the books? Troy sniggered, the action making the contact between his groin and Xander's hard body even more intense. "I'm not sure they'd miss us."

Xander laughed. "Neither am I. But Eric's been my best friend for a very long time and I don't want to just abandon him."

"Fair enough." Troy couldn't deny he felt the same about his friendship with Lorcan. Besides, there was something enticing about taking it slowly. He loved the anticipation coursing through his veins, keeping him on edge. After the gradual build-up of attraction and lust over the past four weeks, rushing forward now just wouldn't be right.

"You still haven't told me what you're celebrating? Or even whether you actually are celebrating anything."

"All will be revealed later." Xander's smile was a combination of smirk and shyness. "It's too long a story to tell here in all this noise."

Troy could wait. He couldn't deny he was curious, but as long as the celebration included him, he'd no problem waiting for an explanation.

When Xander pulled back and announced he wanted another drink before leaving, Troy had no idea how long they had been dancing.

"You go order a round of drinks while I take a leak. I'll join up with you at the bar."

"Sure." Xander pulled Troy close again and smashed their mouths together. Tongues tangled and fought until Troy thought he'd pass out from lack of oxygen.

"Bastard," Troy muttered the word affectionately as Xander pulled away and walked in the direction of the bar. Pushing his way through the crowds as fast as he could, he headed to the toilets, hoping he'd make it in and out quickly. Even a few minutes away from Xander suddenly felt like time wasted.

Chapter Twenty-One

Xander caught a glimpse of himself and the stupid grin on his face in a mirror as he walked to the bar. He didn't care nor did he try to hide it. He'd heard the word Troy had muttered and had accepted it as the endearment he knew it to be. How miraculous that Troy would be as impatient and aroused as Xander was. That was as wondrous as discovering that Troy was the exception to prove the rule — a man looking for more than just instant gratification.

Not much longer now. Just another hour or so. The words sang through Xander's head.

As he waited at the crowded bar for his turn to be served he reflected that he wasn't sure why he hadn't agreed to Troy's suggestion to leave now. He'd been counting down first the weeks, then the days and finally the hours before he would at last be able to just let go with Troy and now that the moment had arrived he'd postponed it. And it had nothing to do with not wanting Troy. He couldn't wait to see Troy's body in what he had no doubt would be all its glory. He'd imagined running his hand over that torso so many times over the past three weeks he couldn't wait to discover if the reality would be as awesome as his fantasies had led him to believe.

He glanced around at the other people waiting for the bartenders' attention and caught someone staring at him. His breath caught as he quickly glanced away only to turn his head back to confirm that he'd indeed recognized the man. *That's the bastard all right.* His hair had been a different color at the time, but Xander had no doubt he was face to face with the man who'd humiliated him four months ago.

Frustrated, Xander averted his gaze again, hoping it would be enough to discourage the man from approaching him. He didn't want this memory in his head right now. Tonight was supposed to be a step forward toward what he hoped would be something better and lasting. This reminder of his past and the hurt that had accompanied it was the worst case of bad timing imaginable.

"Long time no see."

Xander reluctantly turned toward the voice he recognized even after all those months. The moment he saw the self-satisfied smirk his name came back to him — Shane.

"It's Sander, right?" The way Shane asked the question made Xander suspect he'd gotten it wrong on purpose. Well, two could play *that* game.

"Xander, and I'm sorry, but I can't for the life of me remember your name." Something about the way he leered at him rubbed Xander the wrong way.

"Xander. That's right. I knew there was something different about your name. Just couldn't remember what. I'm Shane."

Xander fought the memories as they tried to assault him, but to no avail. The evening he'd allowed Shane to pick him up was back in all its inglorious detail. What had begun as a fun evening of flirting and teasing had ended on a very bitter note when Shane had gotten dressed and walked away almost as soon as he'd finished fucking Xander. But even that had been nothing compared to the disparaging remarks Shane had made while they'd been fucking or the contempt in his eyes when Xander had suggested exchanging telephone numbers.

'God save me from needy bottoms.' Just remembering the words made the humiliation flare up again. *'Don't flatter yourself,'* Shane had continued at the time. *'Even if I wasn't leaving tomorrow there'd be no follow up. You're a tight hole for the night, nothing more and nothing less.'*

That had been the hook-up to leave a dirty taste in Xander's mouth. The first time he'd had no doubt he'd been used, even if he had been a willing participant in the proceedings. He hadn't stopped sleeping around after that night, but from that moment forward he'd wondered if everybody recognized him as needy and took that as an excuse to try to take advantage of him.

Xander looked over Shane's shoulder, hoping to see Troy coming his way but there was no sign of him. He really didn't want to talk to Shane now. He was in the middle of what showed every sign of turning into his best evening in a very long time, and the last thing he needed was Shane reminding him of nights he'd rather forget.

"So, are you surprised to see me again?" Shane seemed as if he expected Xander to be over the moon about their reunion. "Or maybe happy, excited even?" Shane reached out and grabbed Xander's crotch. "Something is hard for me."

Xander almost laughed out loud. His cock had indeed still been hard as a result of his dancing with Troy and the fantasies running through his head about what the two of them might get up to later. Under Shane's attention the excitement, as well as the hard-on wilted. It was all Xander could do not to violently push Shane away but he didn't want to create a scene or risk being thrown out of the club. Not without Troy anyway.

"Leave it, okay? Like you said at the time, once was enough."

"Don't be a spoilsport." Shane's speech slurred a bit, enhancing Xander's worry about what might come next. Reasoning with inebriated men was a lost cause in his experience, and Shane didn't appear as if he would disprove that rule. Shane pushed himself closer to Xander and he wondered how to dislodge him again without creating a scene. If only Troy would show up right now it would make the whole situation so much easier.

"Bugger off! I'm here with someone, and even if I wasn't I wouldn't be interested in a repeat performance." Xander didn't care whether he sounded rude or not. He just wanted

Shane to disappear again.

"You don't mean that." The smile on Shane's face was probably meant to be seductive and cute but came across as arrogant. "Don't you remember how good it was? I do." Shane pushed himself closer to Xander again.

Pressed in by the other people waiting around the bar, Xander had nowhere to retreat to.

"You looked so cute with your arse in the air, waiting for me to fill you." Shane's hand was back on Xander's crotch, squeezing what had ceased to be a stiff cock. Even Xander's obvious lack of physical interest didn't deter Shane. "Never mind who you came here with. You've got me now and you know I'm good."

Anger erupted inside Xander. He pushed his face close to Shane's and opened his mouth to give the persistent little pest a piece of his mind.

"What the fuck?" Troy's outraged voice managed what none of Xander's words and actions had been able to accomplish as Shane hastily stepped back.

"I don't fucking believe it. From him" — Troy glared at Shane — "it doesn't surprise me. But you —" He turned his attention to Xander. "You had actually managed to convince me you were different. I must be stupid because I trusted you. And now you and him are all over each other? Well, fuck you."

Before Xander had time to take a breath, never mind formulate a response, Troy turned around and stalked away. Xander took a step to follow him when a hand on his upper arm held him back.

"Let him go. He's a drama queen."

Xander turned to Shane, fury rushing through him. He'd no idea what had just happened or why Troy had been so angry but he'd no doubt that whatever it was, Shane was the cause of all of it. Without thinking and not caring about the possible consequences, Xander grabbed Shane by the throat, the urge to hit him almost irresistible. He glanced at his hand, squeezing Shane's neck, and saw the tattoo.

Patience. If he'd ever needed to keep himself under control, it was now. For all the satisfaction beating up Shane might give him, his priority right now was to follow Troy and sort this mess out. But first he needed answers. Xander loosened his grip by a fraction and pushed in closer to Shane.

"What just happened? Why is he so angry? How do you know Troy?" He shot the questions off, one after another, without giving Shane the opportunity to reply. "I hope you have good answers 'cause I'm fit to kill you right now." As he spoke a nasty suspicion sprang up in his mind and he hoped against hope he was wrong.

The teasing, flirtatious gleam faded from Shane's eyes to be replaced by something closely resembling fear.

"Cool it, man. That's just Troy being Troy. He can be a bit oversensitive. He's easily hurt. He'll get over it."

"What exactly will he get over? Because as far as you and I are concerned there's nothing to get over."

"He's had a thing for me for years." Selfish pride flashed across Shane's face before disappearing again. "Not that anything ever happened of course. He's so not my type."

Xander glared at Shane. "There's more. What are you not telling me?"

Shane deflated before Xander's eyes. Any trace of smugness vanished as Shane tried to pull away.

"Spill." Xander tightened his grip on Shane.

Shane glanced to the side before answering, "We were sorta supposed to go into business together when I got the offer to work in Florida." Shane looked back at Xander with renewed bravado. "What was I supposed to do? It was and still is the best opportunity I've ever had. I couldn't refuse the offer just because he'd already signed the lease on the shop."

Xander released Shane as his worst fears were confirmed and the reality of the situation crashed into him. No wonder Troy had been upset. It must have been so hurtful to see Xander up close and, what would probably have appeared to be, personal with the man who had betrayed him. *Shit, bollix, fuck.* He had to go and find Troy and explain that no matter what it had looked like, he'd misinterpreted the situation. He took a step back, and turned toward the exit before realizing he had to say something to Eric and Lorcan before rushing after Troy. Without sparing Shane another word, he strode away toward the seating area where the two men were still in deep conversation despite the noise and crowded conditions.

"Hey, you took your time. I was sure you and Troy had snuck off together. Where's…" Eric's voice trailed off as he studied Xander's face. "What's wrong? Where is Troy?"

"I don't know." Xander had no idea where to start and didn't want to have this conversation in the club with people dancing around him while trying to shout over the music. "I'd hoped he might be here. There was a misunderstanding. I have to go and find him."

Just before he walked toward the exit, Xander noticed both Lorcan and Eric opening their mouths to ask him questions but he didn't have the time. He had to get to Troy and resolve this unfortunate mess. Surely it was just a not so minor blip, and not something they wouldn't be able to overcome.

Outside the club Xander took a moment to look up and down the street, hoping for a glimpse of Troy only to find none. A hand landed on his shoulder and Xander didn't need to turn around to guess who it belonged to. "I wouldn't rush after him if I were you. Troy's very good at holding grudges. He's made up his mind now and you'll never convince him he's wrong."

Xander studied the smirk that had returned to Shane's face while clenching his hands in an effort not to hit him.

"He was there that evening I went home with you. I'm sure he hoped I'd spend the night with him but like I said, he so not my type."

Xander stared at Shane, his mind a whirlpool of disconnected but desperate thoughts. *Shit.* How had he forgotten? Troy resting against the wall on the far side of the club, with his arms crossed over his chest, staring at Shane and Xander when they left.

All the rage he'd been trying to keep under control exploded into a bright red haze of fury as he realized how angry, betrayed, and hurt Troy had to feel. Without a moment's hesitation, he pulled back his fist and slammed it into Shane's nose.

Some situations couldn't be solved using patience.

"Hey, you!"

Xander heard the shouting but ignored it as he walked away as fast as he could without actually running. He didn't look back to see if the bouncer was following him or to find out how Shane was doing. His only plan was to find Troy, explain what had happened and fix the situation. *Surely I can fix this.*

Xander clung to the hope that a conversation would clear up the mess Shane had created. He tried calling Troy but wasn't surprised when the phone went straight to voicemail. His text messages went unanswered as well, deepening Xander's worry. His heart sank when he found the shop shrouded in darkness. He remembered seeing traces of light emerging through the seams between the internal door and its frame the night he'd had dinner with Troy. Had Troy not gone home or had he left the lights off on purpose?

Xander rang the bell and when that had no result banged on the door. Kneeling down he opened the letter box and shouted through it.

"Troy, open the door. Please, if you're there, just let me in. Listen to me. You've got it all wrong. Let me explain. Please."

"Hey, you fuckwit. It's the middle of the night. Some of us want to sleep. Fuck off before I call the guards."

The angry voice erupting from one of the windows belonging to the apartment above Troy's, forced Xander to reconsider his actions. If Troy was behind that locked door he clearly didn't want to talk to Xander. If he wasn't there Xander was disturbing the neighborhood for no good reason. Either way he was wasting his breath.

"You're right. I'm sorry." He looked up at the man hanging out of the opened window above him, turned and walked away.

Chapter Twenty-Two

A nagging pain in his neck and both his arms heavy with pins and needles were the first things Troy was aware of when he woke up. He lifted his head from its uncomfortable position on his folded arms on the kitchen table and stared at his surroundings through bleary eyes. For a few short and blissful moments, he had no idea what had possessed him to fall asleep sitting at the table, then memories crashed in and it was all he could do not to drop his head back to its former position and search for the oblivion of sleep once again. Not that he'd any hope of finding that escape again now that his mind was ablaze with images and sounds from the night before.

The last thing he remembered was listening to the ringing of his front door bell, the banging on his door and Xander's loud voice pleading with him. He hadn't been able to react or move. He'd sat at the table, frozen, as if ice was running through his veins, leaving him stiff, cold and immobile. He grimaced. His body was as rigid as it had been before he'd embraced the intermittent darkness, except now it had nothing to do with cold despair. Quite the opposite, in fact. Right now his blood appeared to be boiling in his veins. The anger and embarrassment he hadn't allowed himself to acknowledge before, seemed to have engulfed him during his restless night. He turned his head and glanced out the kitchen window. The world looked as gray and forlorn as his life had once again become.

Standing, he shook his hands. The tingling in his arms got worse as the heaviness receded and he waited for the pain that always followed a severe case of pins and needles to start. As desperate as he was for coffee he didn't dare make one yet. Until his circulation returned to normal it wouldn't be safe to pick things up, especially not if it involved boiling water.

What the fuck had happened? How had he gone from festive and happy to furious in ten seconds flat? *Shane*. Once again it had been Shane. How was it possible for that man to destroy everything which might have been a positive in Troy's life? Months of leading him on while never having any intention to act on it hadn't been enough. Leaving Troy stranded with a shop he was struggling to run on his own had not been the end of it, either. Just when Troy had started to see light and hope in his life again, the bastard had returned to take that away as well.

With the blood flow in his arms finally back to normal, Troy filled the kettle and turned it on. Of course there'd been two men involved this time around. As he poured hot water on the coffee granules in his mug Troy realized he wasn't sure who he was more disappointed with, Xander or himself. He'd been so sure about Xander. He'd allowed himself to believe that at last he'd found a man he could trust. Someone who was really interested in him, Troy, for who he was, and not because they needed something from him. He'd even told himself that Xander's reluctance to push the attraction between them into sex meant that Xander was serious about aiming for something beyond a fling. More fool him.

As he sipped his coffee, he had to admit he was most frustrated with himself. He'd vowed he'd never allow anyone to betray his trust again. He'd really believed he'd learned his lesson after the whole mess with Shane. Yet, here he was again. Alone and devastated.

He picked up his phone and turned it back on. He'd switched it off as soon as he left the club the night before, unwilling and unable to deal with whatever Xander or anybody else might have to say about what had happened — what he'd seen.

He closed his eyes and the image was back. Xander and Shane up close and personal—almost nose to nose, as if they'd been moments away from kissing. Swallowing hard, he forced his eyes open again and concentrated on the furiously blinking phone in his hand. The list of missed calls was long. He saw several from Lorcan and realized he'd have to react to them soon. He'd no intention of doing anything about the numerous calls from Xander, the last one less than twenty minutes ago. He ignored them, as he did the endless list of text messages Xander had sent him. It didn't matter what he had to say, whatever excuses he might be able to come up with. Troy had no doubt what he had seen and he didn't need to be a genius to figure out what it meant. After all, he'd witnessed Shane and Xander leave a party together before. Xander had probably decided it was better to stick with the devil he knew than try his luck on somebody new.

When his phone started ringing Troy nearly dropped it. He had his thumb poised to hit the reject button when he saw Lorcan's name on the screen.

"Hello."

"Well, thank God for that." There was no mistaking the relief in Lorcan's voice. "I was starting to fear you'd fallen off the edge of the world. Are you at home?"

"Yeah, but..."

"Right. I'll be there in fifteen minutes and don't even think about not letting me in."

The connection was severed before Troy had the opportunity to tell Lorcan he'd rather be on his own. Not that it would have made a damn bit of difference if he had been able to get the words out. He knew his friend. Once Lorcan got an idea in his head he turned into an unstoppable force. Resigned to his fate and recognizing that he probably needed to talk to someone, Troy pushed away from the table. He needed a quick shower and fresh clothes. He'd no doubt he stank and he didn't want to wear an outfit that reminded him of everything that had gone wrong last night.

"Where'd you go, man?" Lorcan released Troy from the hug he'd enveloped him in as soon as he'd walked through the door and stepped back, looking at Troy with a frown and concern clear on his face. "You had us worried sick."

As soon as Lorcan retreated, Troy missed his arms around him. He'd found momentary peace in his friend's embrace while allowing his head to rest on the one pair of shoulders he'd always been able to trust.

"Us?"

"Yes, of course. Me, Eric and Xander. We'd no idea where you'd gone or why. Xander was frantic. I've never seen a man leave a club in such haste. He's been calling me all night, trying to find out where you are and if you are okay. And, of course, I couldn't tell him, seeing how you had your phone switched off."

Anger surged through Troy. "Xander was frantic, was he? That's rich seeing I wouldn't have gone anywhere if it hadn't been for him and Shane."

"Yeah," Lorcan said. "Xander mentioned that."

"He did, did he? And what did he say? Did he have any good excuses? Did he explain why he strung me along for a month only to drop me the moment I started to believe there might actually be something real between us?"

"Troy, calm down. You're jumping to conclusions."

"Of course I am. Stupid me got it wrong again, did I?" The words exploded from Troy's mouth as all the anger and frustration reached boiling point. "There's nothing wrong with my eyes, Lorcan. Maybe I'm naïve. Perhaps I'm too trusting but if there's one thing I'm not, it's blind. I saw the two of them. They were standing so close their bodies were almost touching. Give me one good reason why Xander would be nose to nose with Shane, close enough to kiss him without either of them having to make a move. Well. Go on. Explain that to me."

It wasn't fair to take his anger out on Lorcan, but his friend was there in front of him and neither Shane nor Xander were. Troy wouldn't have been able to stop the angry flow of words to save his life.

"To stop himself from smashing the man's face in."

"I don't care. It's just excuses. He…" Troy stopped when Lorcan's words at last sank in. "To stop himself from doing what?"

"Let's sit." Lorcan touched Troy's shoulder and steered him toward his couch. "I'm going to make us coffee and then we're going to have a talk."

Troy's mind spun as he listened to Lorcan rummaging through his kitchen. What if he had been wrong? What if it hadn't been Xander's behavior but his overreaction which had destroyed what might have been? He could probably learn to live with the knowledge that he'd yet again picked the wrong man. He'd no idea how he'd forgive himself if he'd sent what might have been the right man packing for all the wrong reasons. How had he ended up in a situation where what he'd seen as the worst possible outcome was better than the one he might have to deal with?

"Here." Lorcan passed a steaming cup of coffee to Troy, who accepted it with a shaking hand. They stared at each other in silence over the rims of their mugs, taking small sips from the fragrant liquid as it cooled down.

"Tell me what happened." Lorcan's voice was soft, his eyes filled with concern.

"I went to the toilet and Xander was supposed to be getting a round of drinks." Troy squeezed his eyes shut as memories tried to assault him again. "When I came back Shane and Xander stood there, in the middle of the crowd in front of the bar. They were toe-to-toe, only inches separating their bodies. It looked as if they were about to kiss. Shane even held his head at an angle." Troy studied Lorcan's face, hoping to find understanding there and was relieved when he found it. "What other conclusion was I supposed to draw? I mean, those two snuck off together on the night of Shane's farewell party. Surely it wasn't unreasonable to conclude they'd decided to do the same thing again."

Lorcan said nothing. Troy recognized the compassion in his eyes and was grateful for it while he steeled himself for whatever Lorcan might say next. After all, Lorcan had spoken to Xander after Troy had stormed off, while Troy had only ignored Xander's attempts to get into contact with him.

Lorcan stared off into the distance for a moment, as if trying to figure out how best to formulate what he wanted to say. "No, not unreasonable at all, no matter how wrong you were."

"Tell me. Please explain to me how I was wrong. I know what I saw and I don't see any other possible explanations."

"I can't. I'm sorry," Lorcan said. "You'll have to talk to Xander. Listen to him and pay attention to what he says. I can't solve this for either of you."

"Okay. Yeah. You're right." Troy reached for his phone on the coffee table in front of him but Lorcan was quicker and pulled the mobile away until it was out of reach.

"Not by phone. Go to his house and work this out face to face."

"But…"

"Just do it, Troy. Trying to talk this through by phone is a recipe for disaster. Too many opportunities for more misunderstandings and misinterpretations."

"Fair enough." Troy swallowed. "But would you? I mean, if you were Xander would you let me into your apartment after I'd stormed off like that and ignored all your attempts to get in contact? What if he's decided I'm just not worth the trouble?"

"You're kidding, right?" Lorcan's eyes were big, showing his surprise. "I've never known you to be a coward. Of course I'd hear you out if you came to explain yourself, even if I'd no intention of giving you a second chance."

Pain stabbed Troy's heart.

"I'm not saying he's given up on you. If my last

conversation with him is anything to go by, that is about as far from the truth as you can get. But I'm no mind reader and I can't speak for Xander. Even if I knew him better than I do, I wouldn't try to be his mouthpiece."

Lorcan got up from the chair he'd been sitting in and rounded the coffee table to sit next to Troy.

"Just go and talk to him. Explain what happened and why you reacted the way you did. I mean, did you ever tell him about your history with Shane?"

"Not in so many words. He knows somebody let me down. I may even have mentioned Shane's name but I certainly didn't tell him I saw them together at that party a few months ago."

Lorcan nodded. "Exactly. So how's he supposed to understand what was going through your head last night?"

Troy tried to sort through the turmoil in his mind. Lorcan was right, of course. He owed it to Xander and to himself to go and talk to him and explain what had happened. If only he could be sure Xander would understand. He'd no right to expect Xander's understanding or forgiveness after Troy had jumped to conclusions and run away without giving Xander an opportunity to explain or defend himself. Troy wouldn't be able to blame Xander if he told him to just fuck off. Hearing those words straight from Xander's mouth would be even worse than thinking he'd been betrayed had been.

"Go and talk to him. Call me if you need to talk afterward." Lorcan's statement fortified Troy. He'd find the answers he so badly needed and if the worst came to the worst he'd have his best friend to fall back on. It had to be enough.

"Okay." Troy went into the kitchen and grabbed his coat from the back of the chair where he'd dumped it the night before. He was vaguely aware of Lorcan following him when he stepped onto the street through the shop's door. Bleak sunshine valiantly tried to break through the winter's gloom and Troy fervently hoped it was a sign of things to come.

"Thanks. I'll talk to you later." Troy hugged Lorcan and pulled him close.

"Good luck and don't worry. You've got this." Lorcan whispered the words before placing a rather surprising kiss on Troy's cheek. "You'll be fine."

Troy wished he shared Lorcan's certainty and clung to his friend's words, repeating them to himself as he walked to Xander's house, in the hope it would make them prophetic.

I've got this, I'll be fine. *I'll be fine.*

Chapter Twenty-Three

"What are you doing? You won the bet. It's my job to do the chores for the next month."

Eric's voice pulled Xander out of the trance he'd managed to work himself into. He hadn't slept all night as his mind went over what had happened in the club. How had, what was supposed to have been a celebration and a start, turned into a disaster and the end of something that hadn't even properly begun? He'd stared at his phone, willing it to light up with a call or message from Troy, but nothing had arrived.

At seven in the morning, he'd given up on the idea of sleep. Fully aware that the thoughts running through his head would eventually drive him over the edge, he'd kept himself busy with chores. Not wanting to wake Eric up, he'd begun cleaning and decluttering his room. As a result three full to bursting garbage bags now sat next to the front door. An hour ago, he'd started on the kitchen. The countertops gleamed under the overhead light and the freezer was defrosting. He'd just started on the drawer where he kept his cutlery when Eric walked in.

"Don't even go there. Just let me get on with it." Keeping the growl out of his voice was hard work.

"No." Eric's voice was soft but insistent. "I mean it. Those were the conditions and it isn't as if it hasn't cost you enough. Let me take care of the house."

Suddenly Xander's surroundings were clouded in a red haze. "Fuck the bet. And fuck me for insisting to see it through until the end."

"Still no word from Troy?" Eric extracted the knife Xander

held in a death grip from his fingers.

"No." His anger dissipated as quickly as it had flared up. He couldn't decide what was worse, the anger or the hopelessness. He should have hit that Shane harder, slammed his fist into the bastard's face a few more times. Fuck patience. Fuck trying to keep himself under control. Look where it'd gotten him. If only Troy would talk to him, give him a chance to explain. Even now, after he'd discovered exactly who Shane was and what the situation must have seemed like to Troy, he still couldn't get his head around Troy just storming off without a word. How was Xander supposed to fix the situation if he couldn't get in touch with Troy?

"Have you tried calling him again?" Eric switched the kettle on as he asked the question.

"I stopped trying at seven this morning." The pent-up energy, which had kept Xander going all through the night, disappeared and he collapsed onto a chair. "If Troy wanted to talk to me, he would have acknowledged one of those missed calls or texts by now."

"Don't give up yet." Eric turned away from the rattling kettle and faced Xander. "Give him a chance to cool down and get things in perspective. I'm sure he'll get back to you. I'd want answers if it were me."

Xander shook his head and stared at the gloomy sunshine flowing in through the kitchen window. The earlier fog had matched his mood better than this attempt at brightness did.

"I honestly haven't got a clue. I thought I had a fair idea who he was, how he worked. If you'd asked me a week ago, I would have agreed with you. Now I'm not so sure. You didn't see the look on his face before he stormed off. There was so much hurt and fury there."

Xander closed his eyes and saw the image which had been haunting him all night. The expression of betrayal on Troy's face was ingrained on his memory and probably would be for life.

"Let's not talk about it anymore, okay? I have a hard enough time not obsessing about it without us going over the whole sorry affair again."

"Fair enough. If you're sure. I'm here to listen if you change your mind."

"Thanks." Xander forced a smile onto his face. After all, none of it was Eric's fault.

"And you're done cleaning." Eric's voice brokered no argument. "Go and do something else or try and get some sleep. You look like hell."

"Okay." All fight had left Xander. He picked up what remained of his coffee and headed to his room. He glanced around the now spotless space, at a loss how to occupy himself until his gaze came to rest on the drawing board in his adjoining studio. He stared at the unfinished image of Troy and the realization hit him like a punch to his gut. *Now I'll never find out exactly how good he looks naked.* He went over and removed the drawing before securing a fresh piece of paper and picking up a pencil. He wasn't in the mood for beautiful and happy.

"I'm going out for a while, okay?"

Eric's voice brought Xander back to the here and now. He'd managed to lose himself in his art and had no idea how much time had passed since he'd started on his new drawing.

"Sure. I'll be okay." It was something of a shock when Xander realized his words had been true. As long as he had this drawing to work on, he would manage to keep it all together. It wasn't nearly as good as an opportunity to talk to Troy might have been but as weak substitutes went, it was the best he could hope for.

"Good. I'll call you later." Eric turned to leave when the intercom bell rang. "Don't worry about it. I'll deal with whoever that is."

Eric walked away, leaving Xander to wonder why his friend had been trying to suppress a smile, before returning his attention to the picture in front of him. He hadn't meant to put so much despair in the drawing but clearly his subconscious had taken over and reproduced his feelings.

"Hey. May I come in?" The words were barely a whisper and shook Xander to the core. *Troy!* Had he come to fight or...?

"Go for it." Xander fixed his gaze on the image he'd drawn. Unable to make himself check the expression on Troy's face, he made do with the portrait in front of him as he listened to soft footsteps getting ever closer.

"What are you working on?"

Never had Xander been as aware of the proximity of another person. Troy's presence behind him set all his nerve endings ablaze.

"A memory." Xander's voice broke as he said the words and he stepped aside to allow Troy to see what he had looked like just before he'd stormed off.

"Oh." Troy reached for the drawing with his fisted hand, one finger pointing out as if he wanted to trace the lines. When he turned away from the drawing board toward Xander, Troy didn't lift his head.

Xander drank in the sight of the man in front of him. He hadn't allowed himself to hope that he'd see Troy again. Having him here, in his apartment had to be a positive sign, right? If Troy only wanted to tell him how much he hated Xander, he could have done that by phone.

"I'm sorry." Xander almost smiled when he and Troy said the words at the same time.

"We need to talk." Troy looked Xander in the face for the first time since he'd entered. "But first I need to do this."

When Troy stepped forward and raised his arm Xander feared for a moment that Troy was about to strike him. When fingers curled tenderly around the back of his neck and pulled Xander close, he breathed a sigh of relief and relaxed into Troy's embrace.

The kiss was soft and undemanding. This was a reconnection, a finding each other again, an apology through other means. It had nothing to do with passion and everything to do with almost having lost something important and making sure it was still there.

The smile on Troy's face when they separated again was as sweet as their kiss had been, and Xander knew the expression was mirrored on his own face. He rested his forehead against Troy's before opening his mouth to speak.

"Now we talk. I don't want any more misunderstandings between us."

"Okay," Troy said, "tell me what happened."

As Xander explained how Shane had approached him while he was waiting to place his order for drinks and had refused to take a hint or no for an answer, he watched a succession of expressions flash across Troy's face.

"When you mentioned this guy called 'Shane' who'd deserted you and Pins & Needles for Florida I never for a moment considered it might be the same man who..." He stopped talking, knowing exactly what he needed to say and having no idea where to start.

"The same man who what, Xander?"

Xander took a deep breath. He'd always planned to tell Troy at least some of what had led to him getting his tattoo. Now he realized he'd have to tell it all. If he'd told Troy about the bet after their first kiss, this whole mess might have been averted. *No more secrets*.

"It wasn't just him." He stared at his hands as he talked. "You see, I always assumed I'd eventually find someone I wanted to share my life with. Then, just when my career started to kick off and I thought I was ready for a serious relationship it turned out I was the only man in town looking for more than quick hook-ups. And don't get me wrong, initially I enjoyed the whole game. Flirting is fun, and hooking up with a man is a huge boost for the ego, but even at the start it was disconcerting to discover that nobody was interested in exchanging numbers, going for a beer or staying in touch." He glanced up at Troy through his lashes and nearly sighed in relief when all he saw on his face was interest.

"By the time I ran into Shane, I'd more or less given up on the idea of meeting anyone who might be interested in a relationship but he turned out to be a whole new level of cynical." Xander hesitated, then realized he had nothing to lose. He had to tell the whole truth. Troy deserved no less.

"The remarks he made when he left hurt me. I decided I didn't want to be vulnerable again. I stopped hoping for a relationship. One- night stands were just that and I told myself that was fine with me."

Xander wasn't sure he liked the picture he was painting of himself. *If Troy walks away after this, I can't blame him.* But he was nearly at the end, so he might as well finish what he'd started.

"Except that it wasn't fine. And I wasn't fine either. A month ago, Eric pulled me up on it." Xander chuckled but even to his own ears it didn't sound happy. "Since he lives here with me, he had no way of not being aware of my hook-ups. He..." Of course, this was where the story became truly embarrassing. "He bet me that I wouldn't be able to go celibate for a full month.

Xander stopped talking. Troy wasn't stupid, he could figure the rest out for himself.

"And then you went and got yourself a tattoo."

Because he didn't hear any judgment in Troy's voice, Xander found the courage to go on, "I thought I recognized you when I first walked into your shop. But I couldn't place you and you didn't say anything, so I figured I'd mistaken you for someone else. I only remembered seeing you the night I met Shane after he told me you'd been there."

"I had no doubts." Troy sighed. "I knew who you were almost from the start."

Xander looked up only to see Troy studying his hands. *This is ridiculous.* He burst out laughing.

"What the...?" Troy stammered.

"I'm sorry." Xander tried to catch his breath and calm down. "It's just..." He lost it again. Emotions collided in his head. Lack of sleep combined with the pain and fear that had kept him awake all night on top of the sheer relief he felt now Troy was in his house, talking to him, brought Xander to a point near hysteria. Tears streamed down his face as his stomach muscles ached. "Fucking eejit." Troy wrapped his arms around Xander and pulled him close. As soon as he connected with Troy, tension drained from Xander's body. His laughter died down and slowly his breathing returned to normal. He closed his eyes and breathed in the smell of Troy. Those arms brought him peace, as if he'd come home.

"I really am sorry," Xander talked straight into Troy's ear because he refused to lift his head from Troy's shoulder. "It's just… We've been such fools. There were a staggering number of opportunities for either of us to have said something that would have prevented this whole mess from happening."

Troy drew his upper body back a fraction without relinquishing his hold on Xander, forcing him to look up.

"If you put it like that." Troy smirked before turning serious again. "I didn't want to bring Shane into whatever was happening between us. And—" Troy glanced away again. "I guess I was testing you."

Testing *me*. Xander had no idea what to make of that, so he said nothing and waited for Troy to go on.

"I needed to be certain I could trust you. That you wouldn't use me and cast me aside again. I guess I was looking for proof that you weren't like Shane."

Suddenly it all came together for Xander. "And yesterday, just when you'd decided you did trust me, Shane happened and you were sure you'd been betrayed again."

Troy didn't respond, but Xander didn't need an answer. It all made sense now, and each of them had been as much or as little to blame for what had happened as the other. He lifted his head off Troy's shoulder, cupped the back of his head and brushed his lips over Troy's. He lost himself in Troy's mouth. Time became meaningless, his fatigue evaporated and lust slowly built in his belly.

When Troy pulled back, both of them were out of breath. "We're okay then?"

Xander smiled and nodded, bending toward Troy again to resume their kiss but Troy wasn't finished.

"But from now on we talk."

"Oh yes. Until we're sick of our own voices." Xander was about to say more when his phone made the message received sound. He read the text and shook his head. "What a coincidence... Not." He looked up at Troy and winked. "That's from Eric. He's decided to go and visit his family and stay there overnight. I wonder what inspired that sudden decision."

Troy laughed out loud and the sound of it filled Xander with joy.

"I couldn't begin to imagine," Troy said, still chuckling, "but I have a fairly good idea how to take advantage of the situation."

Chapter Twenty-Four

Relief flowed through Troy as he drank in the sight of Xander, nearly overwhelming him. He still chuckled softly but it no longer had anything to do with what he'd said. Ecstasy and anxiety rolled through his stomach, leaving him with a feeling bordering on sickness. He'd been so sure they'd reached their end before even having had the opportunity to begin, that he wasn't ready for what was coming next. He wanted it as badly as he'd ever wanted anything and then some, but he'd not prepared himself for this eventuality. His best-case scenario while walking to Xander's house had been that they might end up on speaking terms again. He'd hoped they would be able to agree on starting from scratch. He hadn't allowed himself to entertain the idea that the reconnection might be immediate, that they could solve the issues between them right away and pick up from where they'd left off before Shane had entered the picture.

"Hmmmm," Xander murmured. "I distinctly remember you saying you knew how to take advantage of the fact that we have this place to ourselves for the next twenty-four hours or so?"

Troy stiffened when he realized he'd been staring at Xander's chin for a few minutes now, completely lost in his thoughts.

"I get it," Xander continued. "It's all a bit overwhelming, isn't it? Only about an hour ago, I was sure we'd managed to ruin it all. Come."

Xander stepped back and took Troy's hand, pulling him along from his studio into his bedroom. Troy went willingly, perfectly happy to allow Xander to take the lead while he tried to catch up with the emotions swirling through his mind. When Xander sat down on the edge of his bed, Troy followed suit.

Aware of Xander's gaze on him, Troy turned his head to face the man. Silence settled on the room and calmness slowly replaced the turmoil in Troy's head.

"Give us a kiss."

Troy lifted his face at Xander's words and didn't try to suppress the soft moan escaping him when Xander pressed his parted lips against his and took his mouth in a deep and sensuous kiss. Unrushed again, they took their time getting reacquainted with the taste of each other. Their kiss was lazy and luxurious, as if they had all the time in the world and it didn't matter what happened next.

Then suddenly it did. As if by unspoken agreement they both deepened the kiss. Troy demanded and Xander gave. Xander insisted and Troy submitted. When Xander flicked Troy's lip ring with the tip of his tongue, shivers ran down his spine. Their tongues stroked and tangled with each other, their mouths pressed together so hard they had to separate for air before diving back in. Hands traveled up and down spines, touching every inch they could reach. Mutual excitement was all too obvious from the sounds and the growing bulges in both their pants.

Need exploded in Troy. The kiss was suddenly not enough anymore. He needed more Xander, above anything he wanted to see and touch Xander's body and skin without the layers which had kept them separated for almost a month.

"I want to see you." As if Xander could read Troy's mind, he voiced the need when they next came up for air.

"Yes." Words seemed like a waste of time to Troy as they both stood, following some unspoken order, and undressed themselves, never taking their eyes off each other as they revealed more of their bodies while dropping their clothes where they fell.

Shoes, socks and clothes were scattered across the bedroom floor when Troy and Xander stopped moving again. Troy fought unexpected shyness as he gazed at Xander and drank in his naked body. The long torso, magnificent shoulders, and slim hips were even more impressive and beautiful than he'd imagined. A light dusting of almost white blond hair on Xander's chest made the pink buds of his nipples scream out for attention. Troy's hands itched to touch all that skin, explore the valleys and ridges created by muscles and ribs but he squeezed them into fists as he lowered his gaze until it came to rest on Xander's long, thick and almost fully erect dick. Troy's cock twitched in response to the sight, and Xander's low chuckle told Troy the fact didn't escape him.

"Oh, God. Even better than I pictured you." Xander's words mirrored the thoughts flying through Troy's head. "Come here."

Troy stepped forward into the embrace of Xander's arms, pushing as close as he could possibly get. Warm flesh connected with warm flesh and heat spread deeper and farther as their mouths reconnected and plundered each other with renewed vigor. When Xander squeezed Troy's arse cheeks their groins found a few extra inches of space between them and closed it. Standing still became impossible. Troy rubbed his cock against Xander's upper thigh while enjoying the sensation of Xander finding his friction against Troy's abs. Only a few moments had passed before they both leaked pre-cum against each other's bodies, making the contact more sensuous and enticing than it had been...almost too much to stand and yet nowhere near enough.

"More," Troy growled the word when Xander pulled back from their kiss.

"Indeed." Xander smiled. "I've been looking forward to this moment for weeks. I want to explore you in detail... and in comfort."

God, yes.

Without letting Troy go, Xander turned him round and used soft pressure against his shoulder to move him backward. When his calves came up against resistance, making further movement impossible, Troy realized they'd reached Xander's target. Xander placed a hand against Troy's chest and pushed. Troy's heart skipped a beat as he fell and the rhythm didn't settle after he'd landed on the soft bedding. Xander loomed over him, his gaze inspecting every inch of Troy's body. Hunger shone out of his eyes before he allowed himself to fall forward, only using his arms to avoid crashing into Troy at the last second.

Xander's mouth was back on Troy's immediately, his tongue demanding entrance to continue the heated dance they'd started earlier. Their bodies moved against each other as lust and heat built in Troy. After only a few short minutes, Troy's balls tingled, warning him of his impending release.

"So close." He murmured the words against Xander's lips. "Don't want it to end yet."

Xander stilled on top of him and pushed his upper body away from Troy's.

"I've imagined this moment, your body, so many times over the past few weeks." Xander sounded in awe. He lifted one hand and traced the lines of the tattoo on Troy's arm almost reverently, sending shivers down Troy's spine in the process.

Turning his head, Troy noticed the symbol on the hand Xander was touching him with.

"What happened after I left last night?"

Xander closed his eyes, the movement forming a frown on his forehead, and Troy could have kicked himself for having broken the moment. Relief rushed through him when Xander opened his eyes again and smiled.

"Actually, I have a complaint about my tattoo."

Xander's words, apparently apropos of nothing, took Troy by surprise. "Hmmm, want to enlighten me as to what that means?"

"Well," Xander said with a naughty sparkle in his eyes. "The tattoo was supposed to remind me not to indulge in hook-ups as well as help me control my temper." He grinned. "While it did serve that first purpose very well, it was a total failure as far as my anger was concerned."

If it hadn't been for Xander's happy face and teasing tone, Troy might have worried. "What did you do?"

Just for a moment, Xander frowned, as if the memory hurt him, and Troy opened his mouth to tell him to forget the question, when Xander relaxed again.

"Initially, I only gave Shane a verbal bollocking. And it would have stayed just that, except that he decided to follow me out. I'm afraid I sorta hit him."

Troy could see Xander wasn't happy about what he'd done. He pushed up and pressed his lips against Xander's before lying down again. "Good for you. If I had done that at the start of the evening, the whole subsequent nightmare might have been avoided."

The last remnants of tension appeared to leave Xander. "Let's try to forget about him. I don't want Shane here He's done enough to hurt both of us. I'm not going to allow him to spoil this."

Troy smiled, more than happy to never have Shane on his mind again if that was possible. His smile turned into a strangled groan when Xander rocked his body, causing renewed friction for Troy's straining cock and encouraging him to move again, as well.

When he'd fantasized about their first coming together he'd imagined blow jobs, lots of lube and condoms, none of which were present. And it didn't matter.

Xander shifted until their cocks lined up before falling into a slow and sensuous rhythm of lower body movements. The glide of two slick cocks against each other drove Troy to levels of ecstasy he couldn't remember ever experiencing without full penetration.

"You feel so good." Xander sighed. "I'm so close."

"Me, too," Troy breathed. "Don't stop."

Xander's mouth found his again and Troy lost himself in the lust coursing through his veins. Shane vanished from his mind, all rational thought left him until all that remained was Xander's mouth, Xander's body on top of his, and Xander's rock-hard cock, stimulating his own organ.

And he came. His orgasm rushed through his body like an unstoppable force. He arched his back, pressing himself harder against Xander, increasing the delicious contact between them in the process.

"Yes. Oh, fuck, yes!" Xander groaned the words, as his movements became erratic. Xander's cum landed on his tummy, combining with the load Troy had shot seconds earlier.

Troy lifted his head and pressed his lips softly against Xander's before relaxing against the soft covers beneath him, relishing the contentment and satisfaction filling him. *This was so worth waiting for.*

Xander allowed himself to fall to the bed beside Troy, pulling him close as soon as he'd landed.

"Can you stay?" Xander asked.

"I've nowhere I need to be today," Troy replied. "And nowhere I'd rather be, either."

"Good." Xander sounded as tired as Troy was. A sleepless night followed by an earth-shattering orgasm had clearly wiped both of them out. Xander pulled at Troy until his head rested on Xander's chest, the arm encircling him making sure Troy wouldn't move an inch. Troy smiled. He couldn't have moved if someone had paid him for it. He was exactly where he wanted to be, and it was all the more precious because it almost hadn't happened.

The rhythm of Xander's heart under his cheek could have been a lullaby. Troy's lips curved upward when a soft snore reached his ears before he too drifted off, satisfied and happy.

Chapter Twenty-Five

Xander woke up with a shock. His arm was no longer wrapped around Troy's solid body, and his chest no longer served as a pillow for a stubble-covered cheek. It had happened again. He'd been so sure Troy would be different, and he'd been wrong. He opened his mouth to curse when warm breath ghosted across his still—or should that be again—half-hard cock, the sensation stirring him like a tender caress.

He relaxed back into the pillow he hadn't been aware lifting his head from, and kept his eyes closed, determined to just luxuriate in the sensations. He was certain he hadn't begun to come to terms with the events of the past twelve hours, but right now he didn't care.

Troy licked over Xander's balls before sucking one into his mouth and lapping at it. A hiss escaped Xander as pleasure shot up his spine, making him shiver. Troy switched balls and repeated the delicious torture before taking his tongue's journey lower. The wet heat on his taint caused Xander to shake lightly in anticipation of what might be coming next. He couldn't remember the last time somebody had taken their time to explore his body like this. He'd forgotten how hot it was to not be in hurry, when there was no need to rush for the finish. When Troy applied pressure, Xander followed his unspoken instructions until he was lying on his belly, his now hard cock pressed into the sheet while he surrendered to Troy's hands pushing his arse cheeks apart, his tongue stroking across his hole making Xander's muscles tense involuntarily.

"So good." The words escaped his mouth of their own

volition. He felt helpless in the best possible sense of the word. Troy was taking care of him, spoiling his body and his senses, and all Xander had to do was take it, enjoy it. When the tip of Troy's tongue demanded entrance, Xander pushed back, opening himself up in anticipation of a sensation he hadn't experienced in years.

"You taste so good," Troy growled, his warm breath brushing across Xander's damp and cooling balls.

Troy's hands pushed Xander's butt cheeks as far apart as they would go, while his tongue pushed deeper, lapping at Xander as he tried to stay still and give Troy free rein. The need to push back, the desire for more, nearly overwhelmed him and fought his wish to make this last as long as he possibly could.

The sense of loss when Troy pulled back and crawled his way up Xander's upper body almost brought tears to his eyes. Troy's hard cock pressing into the crack between his buttocks while Troy's lips found the corner of Xander's mouth, nearly overwhelmed him. Xander turned his head until his mouth fully connected with Troy's and he relished the slightly bitter taste he found on Troy's tongue.

"Tell me what you want," Troy demanded.

"You. Inside."

Troy's answering groan felt like a reward. "And me later?"

Xander almost laughed. They'd spent almost a month dancing around each other, trying to keep a handle on the lust and attraction flowing between them, and they'd never discussed their preferences. "Yes, you later. We'll share it all."

Troy's mouth was back on his, plundering, tasting, demanding and giving. When the tiny ring in Troy's lip hit Xander's teeth he bit down and pulled softly, earning him a full body shudder from Troy. The resulting movement of Troy's cock in his crack drew a soft curse from Xander's lips. There was so much to learn, to explore, to experience, and they had all the time in the world. Nobody was about to walk away. Whatever they didn't get to do today they could do tomorrow, or next week, or next month, or… Xander clamped down on his thoughts before they got too carried away, and surrendered to pleasure again as Troy moved down his body, leaving licks and nips along his way to where Xander ached with need.

Blindly, Xander reached to his right, while he still had enough operating brain cells to function, and opened the drawer by touch. He breathed a sigh of relief when his hand found the lube and strip of condoms. His sigh became a hiss the instant Troy applied his tongue to Xander's hole again as he dumped the supplies on the bed.

Troy never stopped lapping at Xander while he heard the squirting sound of lube being expelled from the container. Anticipation and disappointment fought for dominance when Troy lifted his head and his magical tongue stopped teasing Xander. He tensed in anticipation and relaxed again when the tip of Troy's finger rubbed across his wet hole. The burn he experienced when Troy pushed his finger inside him was sharper than he'd expected and it took him a second to realize that it was probably the result of a month's worth of celibacy.

"Tight." Satisfaction rang through Troy's voice. "You're going to feel so good around me."

"Oh. Fuck. Yes." Xander didn't care about the need ringing out in his voice. He'd happily beg if that was what it took. All his attention was centered on a tiny part of his body, and Troy's finger slowly pushing in and out of it.

"Oh, you beauty." The heat in Troy's voice as he stroked his free hand over the globes of Xander's arse was breathtaking. "Help me out here. Open up for me."

With his head and chest resting on the bed, his arse up in the air and his hands spreading his buttocks, Xander knew he was the poster child for wanton need, which was fine because red hot desire coursed through his veins. The yearning to have Troy hammer into him nearly overwhelmed him. He didn't want to wait, didn't care whether or not Troy prepared him properly as long as he pushed that cock deep inside and owned Xander.

A second well-lubed finger joined the first. Again the burn, but already less pronounced. Xander rocked on the fingers, silently begging for more.

"Needy." The teasing note in Troy's voice almost got lost as his hunger sounded through loud and clear.

A third finger spread Xander wide, but did nothing to alleviate his desire for more. Nothing would be enough until he'd have Troy's cock pounding his arse, his balls slamming against Xander's skin. He felt empty and exposed when Troy withdrew his hand. The only thing stopping him from complaining out loud was the tearing sound indicating that Troy had opened a condom wrapper. Xander twisted his neck and was just in time to see Troy stroke a well-lubed hand over his now covered cock with long, languid strokes.

"You want this?"

Xander almost salivated at the idea that he was now only moments away from getting his wish fulfilled at last. It might only have been minutes but he needed Troy as if he'd been waiting forever for this moment to arrive.

Xander held his breath as he watched Troy move in, a hand wrapped around the base of his cock. The hard tip against his hole felt too big, but then he took it. The slight burn didn't come as a surprise and was welcome. He yearned to experience this in full. He wanted the sensations to race through his body, make his nerve endings scream and leave him a helpless puddle of need.

Troy took his time and Xander concentrated on following every inch of his lover as it disappeared inside his body.

"God, but you feel good," Troy groaned. Hands gripped Xander's hips tightly as Troy slowly withdrew until all but the tip of his cock had left Xander's body again. When he pushed back in there was nothing slow or careful about the move.

"Yes. Like that. Hard."

Xander had a moment to be grateful Eric wasn't home.

If his friend had complained that his encounters had been loud in the past, he'd have been shocked at the noises coming from Xander's room now. Xander didn't even try to hold back the groans and growls escaping his mouth and Troy, much to Xander's delight, was at least as noisy as he was.

Troy moved faster, pounded harder, and Xander moved with him, meeting him stroke for forceful stroke. When Troy tilted Xander's body a fraction his cock hit Xander's gland exactly the right way and he imagined he might explode. "There. Right there. More." He didn't know whether he was begging or demanding and didn't care. Troy gave him what he needed every single time he pushed in.

It had been years since Xander had come without having his dick stimulated. The thought flew through his mind that he could try to lower his body so his member would rub off the bedding, when he realized there was no need. His cock leaked pre-cum and bounced against his belly in a rhythm matching Troy's trusts and it was too good, too much, he was so very fucking close.

"Not gonna last," Troy growled.

"Don't," Xander answered, incapable of more words and hoping that Troy would get his meaning.

As Troy's movements became harder and less rhythmic, Xander's balls drew up. He was there, on the edge. All it would take was one good push… Troy hit Xander's prostrate again and Xander's world imploded. Cum splashed against his belly as the contractions of his arse made Troy's cock feel even bigger than it actually was.

"Yesssssss." Troy's rhythm was gone, and as Xander began to still again, Troy exploded his load into the condom.

A few erratic pushes later, Troy released his grip on Xander's hip and Xander realized he'd find bruises there later. A weak smile spread across his face as Troy collapsed, allowing himself to fall onto Xander's back. Xander stretched his legs out and dropped to the mattress, not caring when he landed in his own come or that his bedding would need washing. Troy's weight on top of him was comforting and gave him a sense of security.

"Fuck me." Troy still sounded breathless. "I knew absence makes the heart grow fonder. I never realized the same is true for the body."

Laughing Xander turned over and pulled Troy close. "More abstinence than absence in this case but, yeah. So fucking worth it."

Chapter Twenty-Six

Troy had no idea where he was when he opened his eyes. His confusion lasted until he heard the soft snores coming from behind him and recognized a warm, and at least partially excited, body press into him. *Xander.*

They'd sorted it out. What Troy had feared might have been the end had turned out to be a wonderful beginning. He shuddered when he acknowledged how close he'd come to losing this because of his hot-headed assumptions. Perhaps he needed a patience tattoo to match Xander's. The idea made him smile. He might do that. Not right now, that would be too much, but a few months from today, if they were still going strong.

He waited for the all too familiar insecurities to kick in, but they refused to surface. Apparently even his subconscious agreed he'd stumbled on to something – or rather somebody – good for a change.

Trying very hard not to disturb Xander, he reached for the bedside table where he'd left his phone before they'd finally gone to sleep. They'd only left Xander's bed for food the day before. They'd fucked again, Xander taking the lead on that occasion, and they'd cuddled and talked. Once they'd gotten rid of the wild animal passion, they'd taken their time exploring each other's bodies at their leisure. Discovering Xander's sensitive spots, the inches of skin which made him shudder when licked and where exactly he was ticklish, had been a sheer delight.

Troy checked the time. Six o'clock. He'd have to get up in about an hour if he wanted to make it back to his own place in time to change into fresh clothes before he had to open his shop.

He sighed when he remembered how Xander had traced every single line of the sleeve tattoo on Troy's arm as if he'd been trying to memorize the pattern. And who knew? Considering Xander was an artist, it was quite possible that was exactly what he had been doing.

He suppressed a snigger when he remembered Xander's fascination with Troy's nipple rings.

'Fuck. That's sexy.' Xander had been fixated on the things. He'd teased them with his fingers, turned them and eventually pulled on them with his teeth while his tongue caressed the nipple itself. It had left Troy a quivering and needy mess, much to Xander's delight.

Troy had no intention of going back to sleep. He was just going to lay here and enjoy Xander's presence. The heavy arm thrown over his middle, the semi-hard dick poking into his arse cheek. He wriggled his backside and was rewarded with a sleepy and soft sigh before he wriggled again.

"Time is it?" Xander croaked the question out, sleep evident in his voice.

"Just gone six. I've got about an hour."

"Don't want you to go." Xander's arm tightened around Troy's middle, pulling him closer.

"Me, neither. But I have this business I'm trying to keep afloat and I do actually have three clients booked this morning."

Xander pulled him over until Troy was laying on his back, staring up at Xander who was suddenly wide awake and looming over him.

"That's fantastic." Genuine delight was visible on Xander's face. "Things are improving then?"

Troy considered the question for a moment before answering. Three consecutive appointments did not a successful business make. But today wasn't the only day in the coming week with more than just one or two bookings. "Yeah, it looks that way. Early days, but things may be looking up."

Xander's smile widened before his face turned thoughtful. "I have a suggestion but you have to promise you won't take it the wrong way or get upset with me."

A tendril of worry settled in Troy's stomach before he nodded his head. "Tell me."

"Remember that tattoo I designed for you?"

"Yes." Troy's worries left him for a moment. "The client is delighted. I'll be finishing the work on Thursday."

"Really? Any chance I could drop by and see the end result?" Xander's enthusiasm was endearing.

"Sure. Is that what you wanted to discuss?"

"No." Xander's face changed again, as if he was weighing his words. "I've been going over what you said. How you don't have an artist to create original images for you and I wondered... How would you feel about...?"

"What?" Despite his concerns having returned at full force Troy couldn't help being amused as Xander squirmed his way toward whatever was on his mind.

"Would you let me do that for you? Draw those images when customers come with requests for which you don't have the right template."

Troy opened his mouth to respond, even though he wasn't sure what he wanted to say, but Xander had suddenly found his tongue and rushed on.

"I really enjoyed doing that first one for you. It's so close to what I do in my own art, and yet it's different. There's an added edge when you draw something which will be immortalized on someone's body."

"Xander." Troy reached out and stroked Xander's scruffy face. "I told you I can't afford to hire an artist right now. Certainly not someone of your standing and fame."

"So you keep on saying." Xander sighed. "I'm not sure how to phrase this so please try and take it as it's meant and not whatever way it may sound." He hesitated. "Wouldn't you let me do it because I enjoy it? Because I want to help you? Because it would be a new challenge for me and I love those?" Xander cocked his head, blushing slightly.

"Because it would allow us to spend more time together?"

His impulse was to say no immediately but Xander had asked him to consider the offer so Troy bit the word back and took his time to weigh the pros and cons and examine his feelings. The offer was so very tempting, if only for the last reason Xander had mentioned but...

"I don't want to take advantage of you."

"You wouldn't be. You didn't ask. I'm offering, because it is what I would like to do. I mean, you could start paying me when your business kicks off if that's what you want. If it's a big issue for you, we could write down the work I do for you now and you could pay me whatever you figure it's worth at a later date. Besides..." It was Xander's turn to trail off.

"What?"

"Well, we're moving ahead with this — with us, right?"

"After everything we've put each other through? Abso-fucking-lutely."

"So" — Xander hesitated again — "isn't that what partners do? Help each other out?"

Troy stared at the beautiful man looking down at him and resisted the urge to pinch himself. He had no idea how he'd gotten this lucky but if the pain and stress he'd lived through thanks to Shane had been the price he needed to pay to end up here, it was more than worth it.

"Okay. We'll try it. But if you get fed up with the unpaid work or I get too uncomfortable taking advantage of you —" Troy saw that Xander was about to interrupt him and pre-empted his objections. "Yeah, yeah, I realize you don't see it as me using you, but if that's how I experience it and if I'm no longer comfortable with it, we'll talk again. Right?"

Xander's bright smile was more than worth Troy's remaining discomfort. Something told him they'd work this one out too. He reached up and pulled Xander down. "Seal it with a kiss?"

Xander's tongue was as soft and playful as it had been the day before and Troy acknowledged he'd never get tired of the man's taste. He was so grateful they'd both stuck around not only for Xander's month of celibacy but also through their near fatal misunderstanding. Patience was a virtue indeed.

Chapter Twenty-Seven

"What's up with Eric?"

Xander diverted his attention from the small, snack filled, plate he was holding, to Troy who was standing next to him. "Apart from the fact that he doesn't want to go back to Canada?"

He followed Troy's gaze to the corner of his living room where a large Christmas tree sparkled festively. Eric stood next to the tree, talking to Lorcan as he invariably seemed to do whenever the two men were in the same room. Xander had to agree. Eric didn't look happy at all. If he didn't know any better, Xander would have guessed this was a memorial rather than Eric's goodbye-for-now party.

"Why is he so reluctant?" Troy asked. "I never got the impression he'd been unhappy there before."

Xander sighed. "I'm not entirely sure. I've been trying to drag it out of him but all I get in response are rather vague statements. Things like, 'it's the middle of bloody winter' and 'I told Carmel next time she could go.' Neither reason seems big enough for the funk he's in, if you ask me."

Troy stepped to the side until he stood in front of Xander and lent back resting his head and shoulders against Xander's chest. "Do you reckon Lorcan has anything to do with his reluctance?"

Xander placed his plate on the mantelpiece behind him and wrapped an arm around Troy, pulling him closer. "That would have been my first guess too. But as far as I'm aware there's nothing going on between them. They get on and are all but inseparable whenever we get together, but to my best knowledge, they haven't so much as kissed.

Oops, we've been spotted."

Eric waved his hand at them, clearly indicating he wanted them to come over and join him and Lorcan. Xander reluctantly let go of Troy so they could cross the room together and zigzag their way through the other guests to get to their friends.

Almost two months had passed since he and Troy had gotten together and Xander hadn't regretted a single second of it. Apart from their first, near fatal, misunderstanding they got on like a house on fire. It was as if they instinctively knew how to be together, how to make it work. Xander could only hope those instincts wouldn't let him down now. He had a question he wanted to ask Troy before the party ended and nerves cramped his stomach every time he imagined making his suggestion.

"You were staring at me," Eric said as soon as Xander and Troy had reached him.

"We were," Xander confirmed. "It's your party. Of course you're the center of attention."

"Hmmm." Eric clearly wasn't convinced but he didn't appear to want to press the issue.

"What's up with you, anyway? I mean this is supposed to be a celebration, yet you're standing here, almost hiding in a corner, with a frown on your face severe enough to scare all but the bravest guests off talking to you." Xander might joke about it but he couldn't help worrying about his friend.

Eric sighed and Xander noticed the concern on Lorcan's face the sound elicited.

"I just don't want to go away again. I've only been back for a few months. I've settled back in, even if I haven't found a place of my own yet." Eric's frown deepened. "Besides, Carmel and I had agreed she would go if there was a need for either of us to go overseas again. I've done my bit."

"So what happened?" Troy asked.

"It's not a new job. The last company I worked with before coming home from Canada wants more work done and Carmel's decided that means I should go back." He shrugged. "She may well have a point, but she could have at least offered to go, instead of being clearly delighted she could wriggle her way out of it so easily."

"Have you told her how much you don't want to go?"

"You bet your arse I did." Eric glared toward the opposite side of the room where an intoxicated Carmel was loudly discussing the pros and cons of magnolia paint with a rather bemused-looking man Xander couldn't immediately identify.

"It's only for three months," Lorcan said in an obvious attempt to lighten the mood. "You'll be back before you know it."

Xander couldn't escape the impression that the words would have had more effect if Lorcan could have made it sound as if he meant them.

"Hey, did you hear about the referendum?" Lorcan's tone of voice changed and he now sounded excited as he addressed Xander and Troy.

"The one on lowering the minimum age for presidential candidates, you mean?" Xander couldn't repress a chuckle at the teasing note in Troy's voice as he answered his friend's question.

"No, you eejit. The marriage equality referendum of course." Lorcan's face lit up. "I'm delighted it's actually going to happen. I'll be getting involved in that campaign if I can."

"You? Politically active?" Troy sounded surprised. "Are you sure about that?"

Xander had no idea why Troy made such a huge issue out of Lorcan's interest.

"For this? Absolutely!" Lorcan nodded. "I mean, I don't trust politicians any further than I can throw them, but that's all the more reason to make sure I'm involved in some way. I won't stand back and watch *them* fuck this up."

"You reckon it will pass then?" Xander was really curious. He hadn't given it a whole lot of thought since the announcement had been made two weeks earlier. Not that he wasn't interested, and of course, he wanted the right to marry as much as the next person, but May was still almost six months away. When Lorcan's face clouded over, Xander was sorry he'd asked the question.

"I don't know. The polls seem to indicate it will be an easy win, but I don't trust those numbers. I can see it going wrong as easily as I can see a victory."

Again Xander suspected he didn't have all the vital information. He didn't have a clue why the usually so evenly tempered Lorcan was up in arms about this particular issue. But whatever his reasons were, now was not the time to go asking for them.

Somebody turned the music up and Xander congratulated himself for having invited all his neighbors. One of them would have ended up calling the *gardai* to complain about the noise otherwise.

"Dance with me." Troy didn't wait for an answer but took Xander's hand and pulled him to the few meters of floor they'd cleared for dancing. Xander had time to register that Eric and Lorcan were hot on their heels before Troy spun him around and he found himself pulled in tightly against his boyfriend's hard body. He rocked his hips. *Hard or on its way to getting there.*

That was something else that hadn't lessened over the two months they'd been together. Troy and he found it next to impossible to keep their hands to themselves. All it took was a look, a smile or a gesture, and they would be all over each other, tearing off clothes while frantically searching for the most serviceable area to pleasure each other.

It wasn't long before Xander lost himself in the music and Troy.

When a slow song started Xander bent his neck and rested his cheek on Troy's shoulder, tilting his head so that his mouth was next to Troy's ear.

"Move in with me." Xander shocked himself when he whispered the words. He'd been trying to figure out a right way to make the suggestion all night, and now he'd just blurted the words out.

"What?" Troy came to a standstill and pushed at Xander's shoulder until he had no choice but to lift his head and look into Troy's eyes.

"Eric's gone again and he's already told me he's no intention of moving back in with me when he returns." Xander had to make a concerted effort not to rush his words. "Apparently, it's part of his deal with Carmel. He'll go to Canada but she has to find him a place to rent before he comes back."

"And you don't like being alone?" Troy's attempt at levity was only half-convincing.

"And I prefer to be around you," Xander answered, not prepared to turn his question into a joke now that he'd asked it. The worried expression on Troy's face set the food and drink he'd enjoyed earlier churning in his stomach.

"Thanks for the offer, but…" Troy frowned. "I can't keep on taking advantage of you. You're already doing the art for nothing and now you're offering me your house too. I mean it's not as if I can afford to pay rent right now. That's why I live behind the shop in the first place." With every word he spoke, Troy sounded more frustrated and angry.

"I'm aware of that." Xander wrapped his hand lightly around Troy's neck and stroked his cheek with his thumb. "But I've got this idea." He stared into Troy's eyes again and chuckled. "No need to look so suspicious. You see, if you were to move in with me, I could use your bedroom as my studio. The light is much better there and I'd have more space." *Not to mention that I would be on the spot if you have another client who wants an original design.* Xander wisely refrained from uttering those words.

"But…" Troy started.

"That way, there'd be no need for anybody to pay rent. I mean I could pay you for your room and then you could return the money to me to cover your rent here, but what's the point? We'd only be adding to the bank's profits."

Xander held his breath as Troy stared at him for what

might as well have been hours, before throwing back his head and laughing.

"You've got me well sussed." Troy shook his head. "You knew I'd never say yes if it meant accepting more charity."

"It's not bloody charity," Xander growled the words.

"Okay. You're right and I'm sorry." Troy appeared contrite. "But that's how I experience it. As if I can't make it by myself and need all the help I can get." He glanced away for a moment. "Is the light in my back room really better or...?"

"Yes, it really is." Xander would never get used to his macho tattoo artist having his insecure moments. "Listen to me, Troy Moriarty. As much as I want us to move in together, I can't afford to sacrifice my art to it. I would not ask for the use of that room if it wouldn't be an improvement."

Troy's face relaxed into a boyish grin, making him look about twelve years old for a moment. "Yes. I would love to move in with you. I'll start packing tomorrow." His features sobered. "I'm sorry to be such a dick about it. It'll stop as soon as the shop starts making a steady income. I promise."

"It's okay." Xander couldn't care less about Troy's insecurities now that he'd agreed to move in. "I do get it, trust me. And one day you'll understand that I'm sharing with you, not making you my charity project." The conversation had gone on for long enough. Xander lowered his chin a few inches and pressed his lips against Troy's, savoring the smell and taste of the man he'd couldn't imagine living without anymore.

* * * *

Shortly before midnight, people started leaving. That was the thing if you decided to throw a party the night before New Year's Eve. They all had to do it again tomorrow night, so nobody wanted to make it too late. Not that Xander had any complaints. The sooner they left the sooner he'd have Troy in his bed...naked.

"I should go too." Lorcan sounded reluctant.

"I'll walk you to the door." Eric didn't sound a whole lot happier.

"You two go ahead. We'll start on the cleanup." Xander smiled at Eric and Lorcan. "Don't look so glum. Like Lorcan said, it's only for three months." Much to Xander's surprise both Eric and Lorcan suddenly lowered their gaze to the floor before turning around and heading to the hall.

"What did I say?" Xander asked.

"You made it sound as if they had emotional reasons for not wanting to be separated," Troy said.

"I did?" Xander laughed as he picked up the first of what seemed like hundreds of cardboard plates. "That wasn't intentional but judging by their reaction, I wasn't far off the mark. Interesting, don't you agree?"

"Very." Troy smirked and turned around, walking to the kitchen before returning with two garbage bags in his hand. "Here, let's get this done and over with."

They each started cleaning at opposite walls and worked in silence for a while until they'd both reached the middle of the room.

"Did you hear the door open or close?" Troy asked with a twinkle in his eye.

"No." Xander grinned, knowing exactly what Troy meant.

In silent agreement, they tiptoed to the open door between the room and the hall and came to an abrupt and simultaneous standstill when they saw Eric and Lorcan engaged in a heated kiss.

They glanced at each other and turned around before making their way to the couch as quietly as they could. Xander sank into the cushions and stared up at his soon to be housemate.

"Oh, dear," Troy said before straddling Xander's legs and claiming his mouth in a kiss as passionate as the one they'd just witnessed.

For a few moments, Xander's thoughts lingered on Eric and Lorcan's bad timing and then he forgot about his friend's problems as he lost himself in the mouth and body of Troy—the man he'd nearly managed to lose, the man who'd be moving in soon and, most importantly, the man he loved.

Scenes from Adelaide Road

Excerpt

Chapter One

I took one step forward before retreating again. The wall against my back grounded me, taking some of my panic away. I stared across the street at the door, the bouncers and the slow trickle of people entering the club. I had waited for this moment, dreamed about it for months but now it had arrived I couldn't find the courage to take the last fifteen steps separating me from the threshold.

I forced myself to breathe slowly while I counted up to ten and down to zero again. My body was on high alert, thoughts rushed through my mind and worry cramped my stomach. This was ridiculous. I only wanted to enter a club, discover what it was like on the inside in order to satisfy my curiosity. Here in Dublin, I had no reason to be afraid — there was no one to tell me what I could and couldn't do, and, most importantly, nobody to frown upon me and who

I was.

I was free at last, but I might as well still be shackled to my father and his rules for all the good it did me. I could hear the contemptuous words my dad used to spew at me whenever I'd attempted to create a social life for myself as if he stood next to me. *'Don't make a fool of yourself. Surely by now you've figured out people don't want to be around you. Nobody likes a loser.'* I had hoped the distance between us would diminish his power over my thoughts. I'd been wrong.

Across the road, two more men entered the club. They exchanged a few words with the bouncers and a burst of laughter reached my ears. I studied them. They looked just like me — nothing made them stand out as special or remarkable. Tight jeans, even tighter T-shirts, and loafers. Nothing about their appearance distinguished them from the people who walked past the club on their way to different venues. Nothing, apart from the fact that some of them had been holding hands and others had their arms wrapped around each other, or hands stuffed into each other's back pockets. Nothing, except that couples entering this club were either all male or all female.

That stood out like a red flag in a black-and-white movie. I couldn't imagine ever seeing that back home. The sight filled me with a longing so deep it hurt. I closed my eyes for a moment and allowed the soft June breeze to wash over me. I wanted to believe I could be one of those men one day. Nineteen years of being told I was nothing — not good enough, a disappointment as well as a disgrace — had me convinced my dream would always be that, a futile fantasy.

Time passed and I just stood there. I had to make up my mind — either bite the bullet, cross the road and enter the club or go back home. There would be no shame in going back to my house. I'd only arrived in Dublin two days ago. I didn't have to hurry or force myself. This city was home now. I could visit this club and others like it whenever I wanted, or rather, whenever I found the courage. I half turned to start the short walk home before stopping myself. *No.* If I chickened out now I might never be brave enough to take the first step. Before I could change my mind again I stepped away from the wall, crossed the street and walked up to the door.

"Sorry, mate, we'll need to see your ID."

The bouncer sounded kind enough, but his words still left me fuming inside as I pulled my wallet out of my pocket and handed my age card over. Looking like a sixteen year old when my nineteenth birthday was months behind me sucked.

"Thanks. That's grand. Enjoy your night." The bouncers stepped aside and allowed me to enter the place I'd been longing and dreading to visit in equal measure.

What had I done? Why had I not gone home? Every instinct screamed at me to turn around and walk out again. I glimpsed bright lights, dark corners and a bar along the left hand wall before I lowered my gaze to the floor. I'd seen enough to know the place was relatively empty. A few bodies moved on the dance floor in the middle of the club and some people sat at the tables surrounding it. The music was loud and the beat traveled through my body, making my eardrums vibrate. I didn't look up while I made my way to the far end of the bar where I picked the empty stool next to the wall.

The marble-like surface of the bar wasn't interesting enough for all the attention I paid it, but I couldn't bring myself to look up, never mind study my surroundings. I waited for someone to come and tell me I wasn't welcome. It had happened whenever I'd found the courage to go out in the past and I couldn't believe the same wouldn't happen here. The setting had changed, but I was still the same as I'd always been.

"What can I get ya?" The bartender appeared out of nowhere, or maybe he'd been there all along.

"Bacardi and Coke, please." I whispered the words and wasn't surprised when I had to repeat them so he could hear me over the noise. I took advantage of the bartender having forced me to look up and studied my surroundings while I waited for my drink. The place was dimly lit and divided into various areas. On the far side, couches and coffee tables created comfortable looking seating areas. Near the door, where people were now entering in a steady flow, and at the opposite end of the large space, I saw high tables without seats. The dance floor in the middle of the room sparkled under the spotlights and steadily filled up with swaying bodies.

The bartender had moved back to the center of the bar to fix my drink and talked to a man while he did so, nodding his head when the man stopped talking. Despite the fear churning through my stomach, curiosity took over. Something about the customer with dark hair caught my attention. He was little more than a silhouette but I couldn't pull my gaze away from him until he turned his head and looked straight at me. *Shit.* Muttering the soft curse, I diverted my attention back to the marble top of the bar and traced a dark line with my finger while trying to get my breathing under control. So much for staying inconspicuous while checking out the club. I fought the urge to look back up and establish whether or not the man was still looking at me. *Don't attract attention to yourself.* The voice screamed in my head and I acknowledged its wisdom.

When my drink appeared in front of me on the bar, I paid for it without looking up or acknowledging the barman. I nearly spilled the rum and Coke as I picked it up. The combination of bubbles and alcohol hit the back of my throat as I drained half the cocktail in one gulp. Tears sprang to my eyes and I swallowed hard to keep from coughing. I couldn't do this. Admitting defeat was easier than forcing myself to be braver than I'd ever be. I'd finish my drink and go home. Being alone wasn't easy but I preferred it over the fear and tension keeping me on a knife's edge right now. Maybe once I'd lived in Dublin a while longer, after I'd gotten a better feel for the place, this would be easier. After all there was no hurry. I'd no intention of ever going back home. I had a new place to live and the rest of my life to explore it.

More books from
Pride Publishing

Book one in the Treacherous Chemistry series

*Like a depressed moth drawn to a wild flame, Chris hoped
that flame would brighten his life, not burn him alive.*

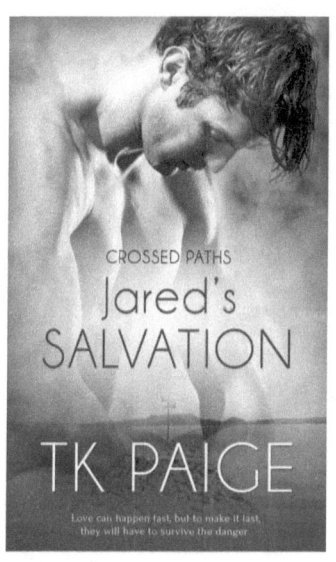

Book one in the Crossed Paths series

Love can happen fast, but, to make it last, they will have to survive the danger that is coming for them.

Book one in The Connelly Chronicles series

Ray and Viv realise love isn't always what they expect it to be, but learning to deal with the road ahead can be worth the heartache.

Book one in the Southern Charm series

*When hotelier Samuel Ashford arrives to change things,
Southern Charm chef Dakota Mitchell fights against it and
nothing will be the same.*

About the Author

Helena Stone

Helena Stone can't remember a life before words and reading. After growing up in a household where no holiday or festivity was complete without at least one new book, it's hardly surprising she now owns more books than shelf space while her Kindle is about to explode.

The urge to write came as a surprise. The realisation that people might enjoy her words was a shock to say the least. Now that the writing bug has well and truly taken hold, Helena can no longer imagine not sharing the characters in her head and heart with the rest of the world.

Having left the hustle and bustle of Amsterdam for the peace and quiet of the Irish Country side she divides her time between reading, writing, long and often wet walks with the dog, her part-time job in a library, a grown-up daughter and her ever loving and patient husband.

Helena Stone loves to hear from readers. You can find contact information, website details and an author profile page at https://www.pride-publishing.com/

www.ingramcontent.com/pod-product-compliance
Lightning Source LLC
Chambersburg PA
CBHW030143200626
46812CB00015B/1017